THE TREASURE OF CHRETIEN DE SARONY

THE TREASURE OF CHRETIEN DE SARONY

The First Chateau Sarony Mystery

By R C S Hutching

Published by Timewarp Ltd

Acknowledgements

With grateful thanks to my son Toby for his patience, enthusiastic suggestions, and assistance.

Contents

Prologue

The innkeeper stood in the bright morning sunshine watching the wagon slowly draw away. The knight's charger walked patiently behind, tethered by a strong leather rein while a mule festooned with armour and weaponry was drawn along by a rein attached to the opposite side of the vehicle.

The innkeeper had no idea what formed the cargo, although he fancied that he had caught a glimpse of gold as the knight checked the rope fastenings holding the canvas sheeting that served to conceal the wagon's contents.

He smilingly raised a hand in acknowledgement of the small boy who, having scrambled atop the canvas sheeting was waving frantically. His other hand gripped one of the ropes that secured his precarious vantage point as the vehicle bumped and lurched along the rutted surface.

Lord Chretien de Sarony had finally returned and was himself driving the wagon. His Lady was seated alongside him and, as the oxen trudged stolidly away, the innkeeper fancied he could still hear her singing as the wagon rumbled around the bend and out of sight.

Now for the pleasant task to hand. He turned and walked briskly in the direction of the village of Colmierre, intent on finding old Auguste the stonemason. The small deerskin purse the lord had handed him jingled pleasantly as he bounced it in his hand.

Chapter 1 - History Lesson

When Professor Smithson-Hunt of the Grantfield University history department called Anna Freemont up to his study she wondered whether it was in connection with the Welsh dig that she knew was in the final stages of being arranged. Her instincts were correct, but she was disappointed to be told that her assistant Rod McEwan was being nominated to head the site work.

"He was promised the next major team leader position by old Professor Thurston, and he needs the experience Anna." The Professor explained, but added "Now sit down and tell me what you know about a certain Chretien de Sarony."

She thought for a few seconds and dredged up from one of the deeper recesses of her mind the few snippets that had lodged there from her time as a student. "Fifteenth century French knight. Didn't he figure in one of those Italian wars involving the Papal States, um he was instrumental in the sacking of a castle, or fortress of some sort? Fros...something or other, oh Frosinone I think. Wasn't there some talk of treasure or something?"

She tailed off as her meagre supply of jumbled facts was exhausted. The Professor nodded approvingly, "Very good Anna. Yes, Chretien was a French knight and like many others he fought as a mercenary for whoever would make it worth his while. That makes him sound a rather grubby character doesn't it, but in fact he was no more or less honourable than most other members of the chivalric cast in those times. We do not know a huge amount about him, but he owned a good sized estate in France, and having fought in various parts of Europe he pitched up in Italy in 1482 at the battle of Campomorto during which he distinguished himself as a formidable fighter. We really get to hear of him, however, as the victor in the short lived siege of a fortified strongpoint at nearby Frosinone in 1483. Following that success it seems that he headed for home and we next find him numbered among the knights who accompanied Henry Tudor to England in 1485. He fought as part of the Tudor cavalry at Bosworth, following which a grateful Henry gave him some land here in Grantfield. He built Sarony House as we now know it and lived there with his wife until their deaths some ten and twelve years later. He never did go back and live on his French estate which is a little strange, but no doubt he visited his ancestral home from time to time.

Seems to have become a confirmed anglophile, both he and his wife were buried in Grantfield. His English and French possessions passed on his death to a distant cousin who appears to have had no interest in the Grantfield property and soon sold it on to some wool merchant or other. It changed hands fairly frequently down the centuries with bits being knocked down and new bits being added, until it eventually became a private school before that venture became commercially unviable. It is now owned by our local council who claim that they will one day begin a restoration of the property, although years of neglect have left it in a pretty sorry state."

He paused, admired for a moment the attractive young woman before him, took a deep breath and then continued.

"Some time after he came over to England stories began to surface of a considerable treasure that he had obtained from the Frosinone adventure. These have persisted through the centuries mainly because they originate from a number of distinctly separate and reputable sources, men who fought for him at Frosinone, a cleric near the French border where he spent some nights on his journey, even an innkeeper nearer to his home territory. These tales have come to light in a haphazard fashion over the years via old documents and registers but they all agree that Chretien de Sarony possessed a treasure that he carried back home with him in a large wagon.

At that point however the trail goes cold as there is no mention in any later source of the treasure being seen, nor its whereabouts. In fact we don't even know what it consisted of, although the fact that Frosinone was owned by Carmino de Fulgese who was responsible for the treasury of the famous Count Florian de Argenta, gives some pause for thought. He may well have brought it to England, or it could be somewhere in France. It has simply vanished from the records.

Now, so much for the history lesson, I have obtained permission from our esteemed council for a low key excavation to be undertaken in the grounds of Sarony House because, being the old romantic that I am, I have always believed in the existence of this treasure. However, because it is such a tentative matter I have been able to wheedle only a miserly amount of finance from the Trustees, and in short I want you to head up this little exploration whilst Rod McEwan is digging holes in Wales. It is a small project and will require a good degree of careful planning.

It does of course promise to be a complete waste of time but, on the other hand, it will afford you valuable experience as project leader. Should you find any clue so far as the Sarony Treasure is concerned I promise to let you follow it through and reap any professional rewards that may result. You can call on department resources and personnel so far as is reasonable, at least until the Welsh dig commences, so you have a limited amount of time before you are down to the, um, bare bones."

Chapter 2 - Anna

Anna Freemont was undoubtedly attractive and intelligent, yet if asked to describe her, those qualities whilst inevitably being mentioned, were always accompanied by comments such as 'a bit up herself', 'snooty', and 'thinks she's God's gift to archaeology'. Physically, she was tall, with a superb figure, and long heavy golden hair, 'a real head turner' was how one admirer had described her. Unfortunately she did not possess a personality that sent out the same signals as her appearance, and a tendency towards being domineering and opinionated had restricted her catches when it came to more meaningful relationships than one night stands.

Maybe it was purely a matter of natural compensation that, having been blessed with an outward appearance most women would kill for, and most men were initially captivated by, she had never felt properly at ease with the world at large. Over her twenty six years of life there had developed a prickly nature that in adulthood sharpened - often with good reason - to a suspicious view of the male of the species, and a stilted ability to relax in social situations.

Now, a week after her meeting with the Professor she strode down College Road towards Grantfield High Street accompanied by a thin faced, red haired man who, being slightly shorter than his companion, needed to occasionally break into a scamper in order to keep pace with her longer strides.

Anna Freemont in full sail was an attractive sight with her long legs sheathed in tight beige jeans. A close fitting top overlaid by an expensive leather bolero style jacket served to emphasise how mother-nature appears to have a penchant for unfairly playing favourites, when distributing those physical assets deemed desirable in the pursuit of an idyllic life.

Anna Freemont in a fury was something not only to behold but to be avoided at all costs. It mattered not that the unwilling recipient of her hostility was also her flat mate, landlord, and would-be lover. Rodney Fergus McEwan was not overly fond of the English, due in part to his Scottish Nationalist sympathies, but mainly from a perceived need to excuse himself from having been born and brought up in Surrey. His hair colour and pale complexion betrayed his ancestry and his slight build -he thought of himself as wiry - was counterbalanced by a hot temper that on past occasions had led him into unwise confrontations.

A fortunate inheritance had enabled him to purchase his own flat in Grantfield and combined with his job in The Department of History & Archaeology at the university his life was close to perfect. Of course, true perfection was rarely attainable, but it had happened to appear in his corner of the academic world in the shape of Anna Freemont. As luck would have it the new senior assistant had been looking for accommodation and Rod possessed a two bedroomed flat. As a result, he acquired a paying tenant who looked like the ultimate personification of his most optimistic dreams, and the opportunity to transform a commercial relationship into something that would make people really notice Rod McEwan.

Unfortunately, the object of his life-fulfilling dream appeared impervious to his romantic overtures, and to make matters worse he had now blundered into her bad books due to this pointless Sarony Treasure hunt. Why bloody Smithson-Hunt had dreamed up the daft project when his own first major site assignment was imminent he didn't know, but he resented the reminder that he was actually the junior just as the promised Welsh project was about to commence. As a consequence he had sulked and put in the bare minimum of effort, resulting in the oversight that had so infuriated Anna.

Her boots squelched unpleasantly in the ooze seeping across the temporary pedestrian walkway that bounded the building site dedicated to the erection of another Tesco store. Her ringing tones could be heard quite clearly berating the luckless redhead as the couple halted due to her suddenly rounding on her companion with the words. "I can't believe you actually forgot such an important item Rod. This is the first site assignment that Smithson-Hunt has given me to head up, and you seem to be doing your best to balls it up for me."

As the redhead spluttered with indignation neither of them had noticed the group of site workers standing smoking just where they had halted. A well proportioned blond and someone named 'Rod' were manna from heaven to this happy band and they were not slow to take advantage of such an opportunity.

"Ooh Rodders don't let her talk to you like that."

"Oi blondie, nice arse."

"Welease wodewick!"

"You know what she needs Rodders!"

Anna's temper snapped and she threw an extravagant V sign at the hecklers accompanied by the instruction to "Piss Off" at full volume, before storming around the corner and into the high street, followed by a cacophony of jeers and whistles.

By the time Rod caught up with her she was almost at the pub and his plaintive "Anna, please, I'm sorry" again brought her to a halt.

As luck would have it they had stopped by yet another building operation, although this one seemed concerned with road repairs and was attended by only one man. Even so, as Anna said "Sorry is all very well Rod, but what the hell are our chances of getting hold of a digger at this late stage?" she noticed with some irritation that the road worker had ceased whatever he was engaged with and was now taking an unwarranted interest in their conversation.

"That's why I suggested coming here to The Magpie. It gets a lot of trade from the local building fraternity and we may be able to hire someone at short notice."

It was at this point that the road worker said something to them that was largely drowned out by a passing bus. She flashed him a warning glare and turned her attention back to the redhead but, to her amazement, the man refused to take the hint and actually tapped her on the shoulder. Her ragged temper gave way, it was bad enough having to endure the verbal attacks, without one of these characters putting his grubby paws on her. What was it with these sad specimens from the building trade that they assumed they had the right to harass any woman they set their eyes on? She spun back to face her antagonist, took a pace towards him, said very loudly and slowly

"Fuck off!"

and marched across the pavement into the pub with the man named Rod trailing a few paces behind.

The Magpie was a popular high street pub; located, as it was, on Grantfield's busiest thoroughfare it had successfully resisted all attempts to shoehorn it into the ill-conceived notion of a British 'café society'. Had the originators of this strange concept made any attempt to understand the country's pub culture, and the fact that the British are totally incapable of drinking in a continental manner, a traditional industry would not have been laid low.

That 'The Magpie' had escaped the transforming affects of internal wall demolition, salad bars, small children running riot, and wall to wall lager was a tribute to the long ago owners who first chose it's location, rather than an enlightened approach by its present corporate parent. As a result, 'The Magpie' was particularly popular with an adult male population that sought refuge at lunchtimes from the doubtful attractions of the hybrid Lyons Corner House meets French Bistro aberrations that were spreading throughout the country. The interior reflected the style of bygone years with low ceilings, dark wood and three separate bars acknowledging the need to cater for varied categories of customer. The absence of the old smoke laden atmosphere was probably the sole improvement, and crusty bread sandwiches still held sway over the invading hordes of tired pizzas and tasteless chips that were relentlessly pushed across many bars. The slogan 'home cooked' had never registered it's alternative meaning of 'only micro-waved on the premises' with the new café society which now got precisely what it's undemanding attitude deserved.

Once inside they quickly found a table in the saloon bar and Rod, who had often fantasised about swaggering into the pub with Anna on his arm, brought over their drinks before heading back to the bar and engaging the barman in conversation. Sitting alone, Anna was conscious of the admiring glances she attracted from some of the younger male customers who wondered how the man they referred to as 'Prof' had managed to attract a woman who looked as if she had all the attributes required to decorate the pages of a glossy magazine. The interest quickly waned as Rod returned and with exaggerated intimacy leaned towards her and confided "Luckily the barman is a bit of a friend, and I think we may be in luck. He says one of his customers runs his own small digger-hire business and he's expecting him to look in for a pint at any time."

He smiled triumphantly "You see now Anna why I make a point of cultivating friendships outside the world of academia."

She hated it when Rod assumed this pompous, self congratulatory, tone and couldn't resist replying "And there was I thinking you just liked to feel superior as an academic among manual workers," and had the satisfaction of seeing his pale face take on a reddish hue.

The moment was cut short by a shout from the bar "Hey Prof, that bloke's just come into the other bar. I'll send him round to see you."

"Prof?" snorted Anna. "Is that what they call you in here? Good job Smithson-Hunt doesn't visit regularly isn't it."

But Rod who was enjoying his heightened status ignored her derision, waved an acknowledging hand in a lordly manner and smirked at Anna, little realising that his afternoon was about to take a very unexpected turn.

Chapter 3 - Martin Price

Anna looked up as she became aware of the figure purposefully heading their way. "Oh shit" she muttered as the man from the road-works paused in front of their table and said in a quiet voice "I thought it might be you two. Is it worth me sitting down, or shall I take my beer back to the bar?"

"We need to hire a mini-digger to start work locally tomorrow morning" replied Anna coldly "Can you help?"

Ignoring the studied off-handedness of the reply the man sat himself down as she cast a wary eye over his work stained clothes. He was nondescript to look at, barely six feet tall, with a decent enough physique by the look of it, but not so powerfully built as to make a girl look twice. The dark brown hair topped a pleasant face although there was a hint of something more forceful behind the grey eyes that now focused on her. His voice was quiet but the words were delivered at a measured speed and firmness that demanded attention more effectively than if shouted over the general hubbub of the increasing number of patrons.

"When you were outside you were shouting like a fishwife at this chap, saying that you needed a digger, and I was trying to offer my services when you swore at me."

Despite the remonstrance being addressed to Anna, Rod decided to intervene and in a tone of voice usually reserved by an adult for a wayward child said "We've already had to put up with more than enough comments from you building workers all morning. Why can't you just treat people with some basic respect?"

The grey gaze was turned on him for an insultingly short space of time before the man took a sip of his beer and, without deigning to comment, turned back to Anna, saying,

"How long and what for?"

Although somewhat taken aback by the blunt and less than friendly tone she answered "Just tomorrow. We need eighteen inches of tarmac and soil removed from a number of trenches."

He nodded and, fishing a slightly bent business card from the breast pocket of his shirt, dropped it on the table. Glancing down she saw that it contained only the company name MM&M Ltd and a mobile phone number. He was still regarding her unsmilingly when she looked back up and said in her best, firm, no nonsense, voice "It needs to be done very carefully, not just as if you are laying a gas pipe in the road, and eighteen inches is an exact figure not a target between six inches and six feet. Can you work with that?"

He nodded and replied "Well of course, most of us humble building workers have moved on to the metric system, but if you wish to cling to our imperial past I'm sure I can get to eighteen inches now that you've pointed me in the right direction. £350 will get you a mini-digger and operator ready to start work at eight a.m. Finishing time is four p.m. All inclusive, no hidden charges. If the job is cancelled before mid-day once I'm on site, you pay half. If it's cancelled after mid-day it's full price."

Anna flushed at the sarcastic response but was about to agree when Rod again joined the conversation. He had been all but ignored, and favoured with only a cursory glance while the meeting he had set up passed him by. Seeing a golden opportunity to impress Anna and climb back into her good graces, he now attempted to do some man sized negotiating based on the verbal skills honed in his student debating days. His nasal intonation seemed somehow more pronounced as he made the uninvited entry into the discussion.

"Seems rather on the high side to me. I'm sure you can do better than that. I'm quite aware of how the building fraternity works – you never find a customer daft enough to agree the first quote do you?"

His voice adopted a more condescending tone "Now let's be a tad more realistic shall we? We'll pay £200 which is more than sufficient to cover your costs and a day's wages. That will buy a few beers down at 'The Buccaneer' tomorrow night won't it."

'The Buccaneer' was a public house set on what was Grantfield's local housing estate ,with a tendency to feature several times each year in the local newspaper when excessive drinking fuelled an outbreak of anti social behaviour. Anna winced slightly at her companion's undisguised disparagement of the man's social standing as she had already noted, with some surprise, that he was quite well spoken. If the implied put down was noticed it was not apparent. All it gained Rod was a momentary contemptuous look from the man, who immediately turned his attention back to Anna with the single word,

"Well?"

Always quick to rise to a perceived slight, the thin faced Scot was not happy at being treated in such a dismissive fashion. The temper to match his red hair rose swiftly to the surface and he sought to further impose himself on the proceedings by saying

"Instead of browbeating a woman why not deal with me. I'm sure the landlord can give us an alternative name if I ask. Don't be greedy, you are trying to overcharge us and you know it."

Finally he received a reaction as the road worker casually emptied the remaining half pint of his beer straight onto his groin area and said "If you don't clear off I'm going to forcibly remove you from this pub you little twat."

Time momentarily stood still as warm beer soaked his nether regions before Rod jumped to his feet with a howl of anger. His chair tipped backwards with a crash and silence immediately followed as the other patrons contemplated the interesting development in their lunchtime landscape. The barman looked long and hard at the corner table from which the unwanted disturbance arose. Unsurprisingly it was the one at which the buxom blond with the nice bottom was ensconced, and he half raised the bar flap in anticipation of having to restore order.

The audience saw the man some knew as 'Prof' standing, with a dark stain spreading across the front of his tan trousers, shaking his fist at the man sitting at the table. The blonde was staring wide eyed and open mouthed at her furious companion, while the other occupant of the table set down his glass and leaned back in his chair, seemingly oblivious to the furore he had just precipitated. The barman stepped through into the public area and then with some relief took a backward pace as the customer known as 'Prof' rushed past him red faced and cursing, and out onto the street. The entire incident had only taken a matter of seconds and, for once, Anna was at a loss for words. The road worker looked ruefully at his now empty glass and said "As I was saying before your pet rodent became involved. The price is £350, take it or leave it, but don't waste any more of my time. I've got to be somewhere in half an hour and I really don't need your company badly enough to make me late."

People didn't usually speak to Anna in quite that fashion and following the departure of Rod – not altogether sadly missed she shamefully admitted to herself – the initiative had well and truly moved away from her. She flicked her eyes across to the barman who was now mopping up the damp chair and floor beneath and was about to reply when the man spoke again. "Look, it's a fair price. I don't try and stitch people up and I resent the implication that I do. My lunch time has so far consisted of you swearing at me when I was trying to be helpful, and your rat faced friend implying that I'm some sort of con man."

She nodded "Yes alright, agreed."

"Good" he responded "I will want a cheque for the full amount handed to me just before I start work. I will then pay it into my bank when I finish at 4.00."

She nodded again "Agreed" and rose to her feet, expecting him to do likewise so that she could escape from behind the table and make her exit. The barman looked uncertainly at the man he knew only as an occasional, but well behaved, customer and hoped that the blonde woman had not brought out a hitherto hidden violent side to the man's nature. An almost comical scene resulted as the seated man remained motionless, arms folded across his chest before heaving an audible sigh and saying "Haven't you forgotten something?" She looked about her for her jacket which she had a habit of discarding and leaving behind, realised that she had never taken it off and, in an irritated voice said "What now?"

He raised his eyes briefly heavenwards and said "I need to know the site address."

The barman relaxed and returned to the safe side of the bar.

Anna silently fumed as she resumed her seat. Damn the man! He managed to irritate her simply by being totally reasonable. "It's the playground area of the old Sarony House School on the A44 heading South. Do you know it?"

His response surprised her. "And you want some trenches dug out?"

"Yes, as I said."

"So we are talking archaeology?"

"Yes, but how do you know that?"

"How does someone like me know a big word like archaeology?" He waved down her attempted response and said "Never mind that. Will you take some advice?"

"Such as?"

"If you are looking to investigate the late fifteenth or early sixteenth century period you will need to remove a top layer of at least three feet, possibly more. So frankly, hiring me to take out eighteen inches will be a complete waste of money."

If the emptying of beer over Rod had been a shock then the road worker advising her on archaeological excavation technique was akin to the Krakatoa eruption. She quickly recovered her poise, just her luck to find a road digger – ha, that was appropriate wasn't it - who was an enthusiastic member of the local amateur archaeology group. She was all for further education which was the route these amateurs usually used, and admittedly they did prove useful when it came to providing labour out on site, but for Heaven's sake! She decided to humour him.

"All our local surveys indicate that the fifteenth century level is reached at about twenty-one inches, so your digger stopping at eighteen should prove adequate and safe."

Again his response caught her off balance. "What research have you done?"

This was getting frankly very irritating indeed and she said in a very firm, precise, tone of voice. "Rod McEwan undertook all the necessary work in that area. All other site surveys around Grantfield support that depth for the fifteenth century."

"Did the rodent give a reason for the playground being over one hundred yards from the old school building, and on a noticeably higher level?"

"Look Mr er, what the hell is your name?"

"Price, Martin Price."

"Well Mr Price if we leave the mechanical digging to you, why don't you leave the scientific stuff to us." That should fix him she thought.

"Suit yourself but this is doomed from the start. I presume you are part of Grantfield Uni, and that they have decided to let you have a crack at finding the long lost Sarony Treasure?"

He took her stunned silence for confirmation and continued with "That being the case your research is faulty in at least two areas." He got to his feet at this point and said "I have to go. What are you doing at say 5.00 this afternoon?"

Every time this bloody man asked her a question it seemed to knock her sideways. "Are you asking me out for God's sake?" she managed to stammer.

"Not in the wildest depths of your imagination," the retort came like a pistol shot, "and when did you last go on a date that started at five in the afternoon? If you would like to look in at my place for tea at five o'clock I will try and save you some money and time." Seeing her startled expression he added "Don't worry, I live with my dear old Mum so you will be quite safe."

He produced a further business card, scribbled quickly on the back and tossed it onto the table saying "Either I'll see you at that address at five, or tomorrow at Sarony House School at eight, your choice! Frankly, I couldn't care either way."

And he left her staring open mouthed at his retreating figure.

Anna took very little time returning to the University, and was relieved to find that Rod had also not made it back following his humiliatingly truncated visit to The Magpie. She took the opportunity to undertake a superficial review of the prep they had undertaken regarding the proposed dig. It confirmed firstly that Rod had been the team member tasked with collating any available ground survey material, and secondly that he had sourced his information and concluding statement almost exclusively from a 1957 survey produced in respect of a dig that was carried out later that year. It confirmed the level at which fifteenth century artefacts were likely to be encountered. A speedy review of the survey worryingly disclosed that it was centered on 'Sarony House and its Immediate Environs' and nowhere could she see any specific reference to the school playground mentioned by that bloody man. That was when she made the decision to visit 17 Orville Terrace later that day.

As five o'clock was signified by the comforting tones of St Bertha's Church bell Anna made her way up the short gravelled pathway leading to the Price family home. She had been surprised at the elegant address that was 17 Orville Terrace, it was part of a Regency building project and reflected the eighteenth century prosperity then being enjoyed by Grantfield. Certainly not the type of

29

accommodation one would readily associate with a road worker and his 'dear old mum'. She was still pondering this when the door opened in response to her firm pressure on the bell-push and Martin Price stood to one side so that she could enter. He closed the door and then led the way along the generously proportioned hallway with the words "I'm glad you thought it worthwhile to drop by" as she silently followed him past a reception room from which the sound of a television could be heard. 'I wonder if that's mummy in there' she thought as they headed into a large kitchen diner at the rear of the house.

He gestured to her to take a seat at the solid looking refectory style table and to her amazement said "Just an ordinary tea I'm afraid, but there is a nice lemon drizzle cake, or some rich fruit cake if you prefer. Help yourself to sugar and milk as you wish. I am sorry that I haven't introduced you to mum yet but her favourite quiz show has just started."

This was bizarre, 'thank God he's not running a motel' she thought as she chose some cake and asked "Why tea at five?" but she knew before he answered that mummy would figure in it somewhere and the reply did not disappoint her. "Mum eats a proper meal at around one pm so only requires a light tea around this time. However this is not a social call is it um Anne?"

"Anna" she corrected firmly.

"Sorry, I only half heard what the rodent called you earlier."

Her temper flared "Must you be so persistently obnoxious Mr Price? Rod has got a decent degree in archaeology which I suspect puts him a touch higher up the educational tree than whatever you hold."

He regarded her silently before saying "What did your site survey produce?"

At last they were there, and despite silently cursing the hapless Rod she answered confidently "We were able to rely on a very comprehensive survey from 1957."

Again his reply winded her somewhat "Which I believe referred only to the school building and garden. Arkwright's dig was concerned only with whether the original fifteenth century house also comprised a chapel as was the case with the Georgian building that eventually housed the Sarony House private school until it closed a few years ago. That survey Anna, did not include the school playground that you are intending to examine tomorrow."

His lecture style manner began to annoy her despite the perfectly civil way in which he addressed her. The best way to defend is to attack and so with this maxim in mind she attempted an escape by saying,

"I agree that the playground was not specifically mentioned by Arkwright, but why does that invalidate our survey when the whole of fifteenth century Grantfield is a little over eighteen inches beneath our feet?"

He sat for a moment as if deciding whether to bother with an answer before jabbing a teaspoon in her direction as he finally responded.

"Had you adequately researched the history of the entire Sarony site instead of doing a half baked cribbing job you would have discovered why the school playground site is located at an oddly distant point, and why it is at a higher level than the school itself. The reason could easily have been found by referring to a pamphlet stocked by the library and originated by the local amateur historians group."

"Of which you are no doubt a leading light," she responded tartly.

For the first time he seemed distracted by her as he said,

"Me? No, what makes you say that? No, what I'm just pointing out is how childishly easy it would have been to find out something that has a major bearing on your proposed dig. You would have discovered that not long after the Georgian building was erected there was a spectacular landslide caused by the unusually high rainfall of 1827, more tea?"

"Y-yes, thank you." Her good manners rescued her from the more modern landslide that she felt was about to sweep her away.

He continued as he poured "The whole of the upper part of what we now call Roundtop Hill became detached and slid down to the level of the road below. It narrowly missed the school, in fact there were no injuries to either man or beast, but the original small school playground was obliterated. The army was called in, the road cleared and the land levelled - although to a significantly greater height than before. The school then built their new playground on the ground beautifully prepared for them by the Royal Engineers." He looked unsmilingly at her before adding. "And that is why any fifteenth century archaeology lying beneath the playground, will be at a far greater depth than is generally the case in the Grantfield area."

She swallowed her pride along with her last piece of lemon drizzle cake and asked "How is it that you know so much about this Mr Price? Mending roads doesn't quite fit your obvious knowledge. You say you are not a member of the local historians group?"

Shaking his head he stood up and said "My step dad was A T Furneaux."

The name rang a bell and she suddenly realised why.

"Do you mean Professor Armand Furneaux, the French archaeologist who excavated Chateau Valette? He was your step-father?"

He nodded and said "Let me introduce you to mum before you go."

'Well that's a novel way of being kicked out' she thought as she followed him out of the kitchen, he really did have an irritating way of simply assuming command.

Anna took a deep breath as they entered the front reception room having mentally prepared herself to face a domineering woman similar to a character famously portrayed on British television some years before. She was therefore shocked to discover the occupant of the room to be a tiny woman whose body was bent like a question mark. She possessed slender arms and legs, and a drawn face with sunken cheeks enlivened by two bright blue eyes. The old woman shifted her position in the large easy chair with some difficulty and peered up at the tall blonde as she responded to her son's light hearted introduction of "Mum this is Anna. She's just leaving but I thought I should introduce her as proof that it wasn't me who ate the last of the cake."

Anna stepped forward and gently shook the slender hand that was held out as the blue eyes swept over her and the elderly woman gently intoned "How do you do Anna" and to her son asked "Why have you been keeping this beautiful creature a secret Martin? How long have you been seeing each other?"

The answer came with brutal frankness before a mildly embarrassed Anna could comment.

"It's nothing like that Mum. Purely business and as I said Anna is just off, but she is a good judge of cake."

"I'm pleased to have met you Mrs um Furneaux" managed Anna as she turned and followed Martin's retreating figure along the hallway and out through the front door.

"It's a fine evening" he said before adding "I'm sorry if that was embarrassing. It was my fault for introducing you only by your first name, but of course I don't actually know your surname do I."

For the first time since their ill starred meeting at The Magpie some of the reserve that he had steadfastly maintained had subsided, and she answered "Freemont. How is it that a person with all this," she gestured to the house behind them, "and a famous step-father, became a road worker?"

Confusingly he replied "I didn't, at least not initially, but mum became ill sometime after my step-father died and so I decided to freelance as a road digger so that I could keep an eye on her for, well, for as long as she needed me. He abruptly changed the subject by saying "The lack of a reliable survey should be enough to put off tomorrow's dig and I will only turn up if you phone me before 7.30 in the morning to confirm you want to go ahead."

She nodded her agreement and then as they reached the gate at the end of the path asked. "Having Armand Furneaux as your step-father must have been a tremendous influence. What did you leave university with?"

He regarded her pensively for a moment before replying. "I read Archaeology at Oxford, took a Masters in Medieval History and gained a PhD based on Knights Errant and their affect on English and French Rivalries in the Medieval Period."

She flushed as she recalled her earlier comment regarding Rod McEwan's degree. "It's really Doctor Price then."

He shrugged and said "Can't stand being called that. Oh, whilst I think of it, don't let the thought of tracking down Chretien de Sarony's treasure influence your decision regarding tomorrow's dig. If it exists it is almost certainly not in the UK."

Despite herself she had to probe by saying "You seem very sure Mr Price."

He nodded and said "Yes I am. Well good evening Anna" and strolled back along the gravel path leaving her to make her way back to her shared apartment, and what would no doubt prove to be a red haired flat mate in a less than happy frame of mind. She looked at her watch and saw it was five minutes before six o'clock. Tea had taken less than one hour but somehow she felt as if she had completed thirteen rounds in a world championship boxing match, losing on points and finishing up with a badly bruised ego.

Chapter 5 - Grantfield University

The playground dig was cancelled, and Anna did not hear anything further from Martin Price until eight weeks later. As it turned out, the Welsh project was also delayed and Anna had been press-ganged into helping with the urgent additional work entailed on what was to be Rod McEwan's first big assignment as number two on such an important site. During that period his obvious attraction to her had intensified until she made up her mind to find a flat of her own regardless of the cost. Her personal life remained in a kind of limbo with no one particularly attracting her despite a number of encounters of the ultimately forgettable kind. Rod not only held no interest for her, but she also now harboured a mistrust of his professional competence following the Sarony House survey debacle.

The Sarony project had been temporarily shelved and Smithson-Hunt although appearing to accept Rod's oversight as mere bad luck - she had not mentioned the annoying road digger's existence - had drily observed to a colleague that the red haired Scot would do well to concentrate more on observing the standards required of a good site archaeologist and less on the sight of Anna's backside.

It was on a Monday morning, following a particularly boring weekend spent evading Rod's attempts to get her to partner him at various social engagements, that she found herself tied up on a long phone call on her mobile.

Her land line began flashing green to indicate a call from the reception desk two floors below and she had no alternative but to frantically signal Rod to answer on her behalf. The modern building that housed the Department of Archaeology and History had first class facilities that included a reception area worthy of a top class hotel and a seemingly inexhaustible supply of glamorous young women to sit and smile at all who approached.

It was to Nikki-with-two-kays that Rod spoke when he answered Anna's phone. The volume and tone of his voice as he said "Who did you say is down there?" caught Anna's attention and the bang as he slammed down the handset and rushed out of her office alerted her to the possibility of trouble ahead. She swiftly terminated her call and phoned reception and was informed that a Mr Price had asked for her, but that Rod McEwan had said he would deal with him and was already on his way down. For the second time in as many minutes the four junior department members occupying the outer office were treated to the spectacle of a senior member running through their work area and clattering down the stairs in preference to waiting for the lift.

Anna's longer legs enabled her to make up some of the lost ground but, as she emerged into the reception area, it was prudent to slow to a brisk walk if only to avoid the risk of performing an unintentional acrobatic display on the ceramic tiled floor. She saw the road digger standing slouched against the reception desk and Nikki-with-two-kays tip her head back and laugh at a comment that he made. This occurred a matter of seconds before the figure of Rod McEwan skidded to a halt at the desk and asked in a voice that was barely below a shout,

"What the bloody hell do you want?"

Nikki-with-two-kays' head swung sharply in the direction of the angry Scot, her mouth dropping open. The road digger straightened himself up and as a breathless Anna joined the little group she heard him say "Careful sonny, your keeper has just arrived."

"Not helpful," she snapped and had the pleasure of seeing a brief look of surprise flit across his face before he suddenly grinned and said "Tell it to Roland here, he's the one with the bad temper. Seems to run in your department doesn't it." The trap had been set and she obligingly walked straight into it.

"His name is Rodney" she corrected, and the response when it came brought forth an inflammatory titter from the receptionist.

"Oh yes of course. Roland was a rat wasn't he, silly of me."

For a moment it looked as if Rod would be foolish enough to take a swing at the taller man when Anna had the presence of mind to hiss "The Prof" and point to a tall bear-like man who was making his way across the reception area a few yards distant. The warning came in time and it was clear that the head of the DAH faculty in the company of two senior lecturers had noticed nothing out of the ordinary. This happy state would have continued, and he would have remained totally oblivious to the existence of the group at the reception desk, had it not been for the roar of "Oi Smiffy" that was hurled in his direction by Martin Price and resounded across the reception area.

An ominous silence descended, heads turned, Nikki-with-two-kays squeaked in anticipation of further excitement while Anna and Rod fixed their appalled gazes on each other. Professor Smithson-Hunt stopped dead, glared in the direction of the group at reception, waved his companions on without him and ambled towards them.

"Oh shit" muttered Anna as The Nearest Thing To God adjusted his glasses and bore down on them. Rod took a sudden and most enjoyable pleasure in the probability that his adversary was about to suffer the public humiliation of being ejected from the department building, while Nikki-with-two-kays found herself wondering if the catalyst for the morning's entertainment was in need of a girlfriend.

Like an irresistible force threatening to sweep all before it Professor Smithson-Hunt drew close and with his gaze fixed like that of the Basilisk uttered the words "Martin you disrespectful bastard! About bloody time you put in an appearance instead of swanning around the world at Her Majesty's expense."

"Now now Smiffy, just because I didn't follow in the exalted footsteps of my step dad there's no need to get abusive. I didn't realise until recently that you'd landed up here."

To the amazement of the immediate audience the professor and the road worker wrapped their arms about each other with the latter saying, "How are you keeping you old sod, still making the lives of students a misery?"

The tall professor smiled "Huh, only when they are awkward buggers like you. So what are you doing here, the last I heard, you were in the service of Queen and Country. What are you doing lurking around our Miss Freemont - or is it our beauteous young Nikki who has attracted you?"

"Well I was hoping to speak to Miss Freemont about a project that could be of interest to you both" replied Price." He looked pointedly at Anna as he spoke and edged his left eyebrow upwards.

"And what role would Mr McEwan have in this project?" Enquired the professor.

There was a perceptible pause before the reply "None whatsoever Smiffy,"

The great man nodded and said."Right, give me five minutes then come up to my study - Anna will guide you. Mr McEwan I will leave you to go about whatever it is you are presently engaged with" and, turning on his heel, he headed rapidly towards the lift.

An uneasy silence ensued as the witnesses to the extraordinary encounter tried to make some sense of the scene that had just been played out before them. Then Anna turned to Rod and said "Better get back to the team

Rod, you can do no good for yourself with any further confrontation."

Price stared at the Scot but said nothing, then turned to the receptionist who had been an avid spectator for the past few minutes and asked, "Ever felt your presence wasn't entirely welcome miss um?"

"Nikki, that's with two kays" she answered predictably.

Rod was still trying to work out what was going on and how come a road mender was on apparently very intimate social terms with the eminent head of his department. He threw a venomous look at the taller man and said "You make me sick you second rate nonentity."

Martin Price smiled icily and retorted "In which case this will be a lunchtime well spent. Now run along like a good little chap."

As she stared at her colleague's retreating back Anna asked "Was it necessary to be quite so rude?"

Price shook his head ruefully "Bearing in mind it was that little twat who was creating the scene, and was on the point of taking a swing at me when you turned up, I thought I acted with commendable restraint. It was you and Smiffy I came to see, not that red headed waste of space. Why not take me to Smiffy's study as he suggested?" Then turning to Nikki-with-two-kays, he winked and said "See you later."

He noticed that Anna didn't make any attempt at conversation either as they waited for the lift or as they travelled up to the third floor, and the frosty silence was maintained as they walked the few yards to the door leading into the outer office occupied by the professor's secretary. They were clearly expected as she wagged a hand at them to keep walking before dropping her eyes back to her computer screen. Anna knocked lightly on the door of the inner sanctum and led the way across the comfortably furnished room towards the professor who was seated on the leather settee. "Ah good. Grab a pew you two and tell me what this is all about."

He motioned them toward the two matching easy chairs and looked initially at Anna who rather stiffly said "I'm no wiser than you professor, I had only arrived at reception shortly before Mr Price called out to you."

"Oh so this isn't something arranged between you then, well come on Martin, what brings you into my domain after, what is it, ten years?"

"About that, I was 26 when I joined the big wide world. You don't seem to have changed much though."

Smithson-Hunt laughed and patted his stomach saying, "I don't think Amelia is likely to agree, but how remiss of me, how is your mother Martin, she was once the life and soul of Grantfield society if I correctly recall?"

Anna found it difficult to reconcile her memory of the little old woman of two months ago with the life and soul of anything, and noticed a cloud come over the younger man's face.

"I'm afraid mum died about six weeks ago Smiffy. She'd been on borrowed time for more than two years - in fact nearer three because she fought so hard that she lasted far longer than even the medics thought possible."

A silence descended which Anna left to one of the men to break and the professor accepted the challenge by saying "I am so sorry dear boy, I have only been in post a few months myself since we got back from Australia, I made it to Armand's funeral of course but have rather drifted out of touch since then. You didn't get to the funeral did you."

"No I didn't, I was deeply involved in, um, a project abroad and couldn't even wangle compassionate leave. It was a bad time altogether."

Anna shifted uncomfortably, feeling like an eavesdropper on a private conversation and wondered just what was so important that Martin Price couldn't be granted leave even to attend a family funeral.

"Yes, people don't realise exactly what you boys have to put up with when…" he hesitated uncharacteristically, and Anna could have sworn that she noticed an almost imperceptible motion of the younger man's head as the professor continued "….. when, um, asked. I'm sorry to hear your news Martin, Amelia and I intended to look her up once we had properly settled in."

Martin shrugged and said "Nothing more could be done Smiffy, let's move on and I'll tell you what brings me here."

This last sentence made Anna feel a keen sense of relief as it felt like hours that she had been sitting dumbly listening to the pair who had obviously known each other for many years and seemed to have completely forgotten her existence.

As if reading her mind Martin suddenly turned to Anna and said "In case you are wondering about all of this I should explain that Smiffy was a good friend of Armand my step father. He was also my tutor when I did my doctorate, so when you mentioned he was your boss I thought I would make an effort and get in touch. Unfortunately mum went rapidly downhill and this is the first chance I've had."

Turning back he addressed the professor again. "I happened to meet Anna just before Mum died and she mentioned your name. Are you still interested in trying to track down the Sarony Treasure?"

The professor nodded "You've got a good memory Martin. We had a postponement recently and so I tried to get Anna here to head up a dig locally at Sarony House, but the survey got fouled up so we had to pull the plug on the idea. It was only a tiny little thing, but it would have indulged my own interest in the subject, and provided Anna with some good experience."

Martin gave no indication that he already knew of the project, and simply asked "Are there any plans to revisit the idea?"

"Unfortunately not, funds and staff are almost fully committed for the foreseeable future. We've got a big deal about to commence in Wales, Billy Carson's heading the whole thing but, thanks to an agreement made by my predecessor, young McEwan's going as team manager. Wouldn't have been my choice I must say, but a promise was made and I guess we will see if he can rise to the occasion. Ironically it's only Anna who won't be out on site for the next six months on the Welsh dig. Why the interest in Sarony?"

"Well I've decided to revive my interest in archaeology ten years after walking away from it. Armand began to take an interest in the Sarony Treasure story not long before his death and thanks to him I've also been able to secure access to the grounds and main house of Chateau Sarony in France. I dropped by today to talk it over with Miss Freemont and see if I could arrange to meet you. It was my intention to ask if the Uni would be interested in turning my trip into more of a joint venture."

"You want help with the finance?"

"Oh no, not directly. I was thinking more of resources being made available in the event of my achieving some sort of success. I have been fairly certain for quite some time that the whereabouts of the Sarony Treasure will be traced in France and not England where Chretien and his wife spent their remaining years."

"You have a concrete reason, or is this just a theory?"

"I have some interesting notes made by Armand."

The professor's interest was perceptively heightened "Indeed, but why come to us?"

"The connection of the town with the Sarony family for one, and if my work was linked to the Uni it would help ease my path back into the world of archaeology."

"So finance isn't an issue, you need something on your CV and Grantfield could be involved. It occurs to me Martin that, with Anna's agreement, we may be able to help."

For the first time Anna actually spoke "How will my agreement to something be of use professor?"

Smithson-Hunt had the good grace to look slightly abashed as he said "I am pretty sure I could get the powers that be to approve a University sponsored trip ostensibly headed by you Anna, but of course accompanied by Dr Martin Price who would be de facto OC the operation." Addressing Martin he added "The only stumbling block might be Anna's fares and board and lodging costs, her salary is already budgeted."

"Supposing I covered those items Smiffy?"

They looked at each other and turned to Anna who felt rather like the proverbial rabbit caught in the headlights. "I'm not against the idea in principle although........." her carefully measured words tailed off and she was about to ask what the dates would be when Price cut in.

"Truth to tell Smiffy, when Miss Freemont and I happened to meet a couple of months ago we didn't exactly hit it off that well. I wouldn't like to think that if she turns this down it will be counted against her. The fact that we don't particularly get along is just one of those things."

He looked at Anna and said, "Whether you come is down to you. I'm proposing a three or four week field trip to Sarony, exact dates to be agreed. I'm taking my car over on the ferry to Calais then driving down to Sarony which is not very far from Dijon. That's about 350 miles, and if you decide to come I can pre-book our accommodation at a decent little auberge in the village, and then we can spend the time pottering about like good little archaeologists."

He turned back to the professor "If however Anna prefers to have nothing to do with this idea of mine, then I hope you might see your way clear to at least lending the University's name to this little jaunt. I'll do nothing to besmirch Grantfield's reputation and if anything comes of it you will have first choice of further involvement."

As the professor nodded thoughtfully, Anna suddenly had the uncomfortable realisation that her presence on the trip had no bearing whatsoever on whether Martin Price was going to France or not. Clearly, with or without her, the trip would be made, and if she declined the offer it would end her involvement in the Sarony project for good. Smithson-Hunt obviously had a good deal of affection for Martin Price, and the old boys network combined with the professor's personal interest in the Chretien de Sarony story was likely to see the proposal get the go ahead.

Stalling as she wrestled with the dilemma she asked "What about French government permission?"

"Well to be perfectly honest I don't think we will be doing much digging" answered Price. "The whole story of Chretien de Sarony is fragmented and very little is known of his movements following the fight at the stronghold. Some people even think that he never got his hands on any treasure, and the whole thing was just a story cooked up by the Argenta family to cover their relative's failure to provide additional funds for the next papal escapade. Admittedly we've got the chateau and it's grounds to examine, but I believe it will be more of a research trip than anything else. If we find some clue to the Sarony treasure then we can perhaps use any ties that this university has with my late step-father's seat of learning in France to help oil the academic and governmental wheels. That will only be necessary in any event if we end up having to dig holes in France. For all we know, we could possibly pick up a clue that leads us right back here, in which case we will know exactly where we stand. Regardless of personal issues I like the idea of having two informed minds and two pairs of legs at the research stage."

He grinned and added "I think we could have what is known as 'creative tension'."

She didn't respond to the attempt to lighten her misgivings and silence descended for a few seconds before the professor pointed to Anna saying "It's up to you Anna, a trip to France or a few quiet weeks as office girl in the department is the choice you have to make."

Both men looked at her and she took a deep breath and said "Yes, alright, why not? It sounds interesting and part of the summer in France is a very attractive prospect even though it is work. Thank you, I accept."

The meeting finished shortly afterwards and as they made their way back down to reception Anna's good manners came to the surface. "I was shocked to hear you mention your mother's death," she said as the lift took them downwards.

He shrugged "She fought to the last, and she wasn't alone. It was why I got Mickey on board so it was all worthwhile in the end. When I first got news of the diagnosis I had to tidy things up, but I got back home as soon as I could. She needed someone to be there with her and you can't just pack your dear old mum off to a nursing home can you?"

As they stepped out of the lift Anna took the opportunity to ask "So who is Mickey then?"

He laughed and said "Not who, but what. Mickey is the name of my digger. Metal Mickey - like the character in the eighties TV series I used to watch. That's why I named the company MM&M Ltd - it stands for 'Metal Mickey & Me'. I originally learned to operate a digger during university vacation time. By investing in Mickey and going freelance, I could tailor my hours to fit in with mum's health needs and spend more and more time with her as she deteriorated. I didn't actually need the money but it gave me something physical to do out in the open, and stopped me going stir crazy." He stopped as if embarrassed by the sudden rush of personal detail then added "As we are going to be spending some time together in France would you like to talk over the Sarony trip at lunch, and I can give you some background to follow up before we leave?"

She shook her head and it seemed to him that her mood suddenly swung from affable to antagonistic. "No need, I'll do my own research and then you can brief me when we are travelling down there. As you are apparently in charge then I'll leave you to make whatever arrangements are necessary. Just give me a call here at the Uni a couple of days before you want to travel and I'll meet you wherever you like at departure time."

He looked surprised and said "I thought it might be nice to get to know each other a little before we go, particularly as we will be spending a few weeks together."

She looked scornfully at him, remembering his treatment of Rod McEwan and retorted "We may be going off on a research trip in each other's company Mr Price, but we will not be 'together' in any other sense of the word. I'm sorry if you now have a lonely life, but this is work and I keep my social life separate." The veiled allusion to his mother's passing leaving him alone was probably unnecessarily spiteful, but it felt good getting one back for Rod. His face reddened slightly as he looked at her without replying. He opened his mouth as if about to respond but instead just nodded and stood looking at her with what was almost a puzzled expression. His unwavering gaze made her feel both angry and uncomfortable, and turning away from him without further comment she headed for the stairs, hearing as she did so his footsteps recede across reception towards the exit.

She was only a matter of yards from the rear staircase when the clickety-clack sound of a high heeled female in a hurry caused her to turn around. She saw Nikki-with-two-kays twinkling across to Martin Price before bursting into laughter at a comment he made to her. They stood together for a moment, she nodded and laughed again, before thrusting her hand under his arm as together they slipped through the revolving doors and out onto the sunlit campus.

As she climbed the stairs she felt a grim resolve sweep over her. If she had to endure the company of Martin Price this summer then so be it. One role she had no intention of playing was that of a grateful bimbo who would giggle and wiggle obligingly in return for a free lunch. Even so, for some reason she couldn't fathom, the fact that he had so quickly revised his choice of lunch companion once she had turned him down irritated her in the extreme. Then, thanks to Rod McEwan, her afternoon passed very slowly indeed.

On returning to the department she had called Rod over and updated him on developments, provoking a predictably scornful reaction.

"The Sarony Treasure eh? I thought that was more a myth than anything else, that bloke bears watching in my opinion. Too bloody clever by half what with all this nonsense about pretending to be a humble road worker when in fact he's loaded to the eyeballs, and lives in some posh house in the swankiest part of town. I'd trust him as far as I could throw him and you'd better watch out for yourself Anna."

"I don't understand you Rod, why should I watch out?"

"Seems obvious to me that now his mother's snuffed it he's at a loose end. Look, he's admitted he wants to get back into archaeology hasn't he?"

She nodded and McEwan stormed on "Well what with all this 'Smiffy' lark and jolly old pals, he seems to have shoehorned himself nicely into your Sarony gig doesn't he? Him and Smithson-Hunt all buddy-buddy with ties going back years, surely you can figure it out for yourself?"

"Figure what out? You're talking in riddles."

"Oh wake up Anna for heavens sake. Look, he's got all the qualifications necessary to be head of department."

"You think he's after my job?"

"He's better qualified academically, he's known Smithson-Hunt for years, he's desperate to make a fresh start in archaeology and, do I think he's after your job? Too bloody right I do, and you've been daft enough to help him get it by agreeing to act as his gofer on this Sarony stunt."

Her temper flared. "I am not his gofer Rod, and if you hadn't managed to balls up the Sarony survey I wouldn't be stuck with going to France with him."

Unrepentant he replied "The Sarony thing was a pure stunt to impress the department hierarchy, and to indulge Smithson-Hunt's personal interest. There is no Sarony Treasure, it's all a load of tripe. We are meant to be serious archaeologists, not a bunch of publicity seeking second-raters posing in silly hats in front of cameras. Why should I have taken it seriously when I was focussed on the Welsh job? I'll be site leader under Carson and if he likes me, and the project succeeds, who knows where it could lead. The old boys network looks after it's own Anna, it's an English thing and it's why most of the world hates the bastards."

She sat amazed at the rancour that had poured forth but deep inside a warning voice began to make itself heard. 'The old boy's network', she had heard those very words uttered in Smithson-Hunt's study less than an hour ago. Perhaps Rod was more perceptive than even he realised. Noting her silence he added.

"When it's all gone pear shaped, and your saying 'yes sir' and 'no sir' to little Lord Fauntleroy, just remember what I've said. Thank God I'm off to Wales."

Chapter 6 - Journey South

It was a full ten days before Martin Price made contact via a message left at reception for her. He had apparently dropped it off by hand – no doubt to the delight of Nikki-with-two-kays - thought Anna sourly, but had not asked to see her. Sealed in a neatly written envelope marked 'Personal – FAO A Freemont' the note itself was short and to the point.

'Anna, I have booked the Sealink car ferry sailing from Dover this Saturday at 9.30 am. See you at the bus stop just outside the terminal. Martin'

So she had to get herself to Dover and then wait around at a bus stop. Well thanks very much, she thought. She foolishly mentioned the arrangement to Rod who unsympathetically commented, "Sounds like something recommended in one of those budget American tourist guides for Europe. I'd watch it if I were you, you'll probably be spending your time in Sarony under canvas - sharing a sleeping bag."

Two days later she stood silently fuming for almost twenty minutes before a battered dark green Land Rover pulled up a few yards past the bus stop and a cheery "Oi, Anna" attracted her attention and the amused glances of a number of other people waiting for the bus. She reluctantly shouldered the bulky rucksack and towed the large suitcase on it's small wheels towards her transport. The sight of a leggy blond tottering the twenty yards armed awkwardly with a suitcase and rucksack was too much for one van driver who hooted loudly and waggled his tongue at her as he sped past.

The grinning figure of Martin Price had meanwhile alighted and flipped up the canvas flap at the back.

"Sorry I'm a bit late, got caught up in some road works outside Maidstone. Here, give me that" and he hefted the case into the rear compartment.

"I'll hang onto this" she said indicating the rucksack and walked to the passenger door and climbed in. Her mood at having to make her own way to Dover, and then the bus stop humiliation had changed her already edgy mood to one of depressed resignation. She banged the door closed and sat without comment as Price climbed in beside her and started the engine.

As they pulled away he explained that the ferry booking was for a vehicle and two adult passengers so they needed to present themselves at the checkpoint together. "After your comment in reception at the Uni I didn't think you would want to travel down with me." he said, then added "Look Anna, I'm not going to apologise for anything that has happened before now, although I suppose chucking beer over the Rode… erm, Rod McEwan was a bit extreme, but we do have to try and get along as we will be working alongside one another." He deliberately avoided the word 'together'.

She looked at him briefly and said "As far as I am concerned there is not a problem about anything – this is a work trip and I will treat you in the same way as I would any other colleague." The tone of her voice implied otherwise, and she thought she heard him mutter "Oh goodie" under his breath but decided to ignore it.

There remained a strained silence between them as having passed through check-in without difficulty they negotiated the boarding ramp and followed the marshal's directions to a parking point two inches from the rear of a handsome Range Rover which Anna eyed enviously in comparison to their own Spartan transport. They locked up and made their way to the passenger lounge two floors above the vehicle deck and he asked "Fancy a cup of coffee or something to eat?"

With a shake of her head she replied "No thanks, I'm going to take a look round in the fresh air" and without a backward glance walked away. He realised that this was the same routine as when they had parted company at the university two weeks earlier and made no attempt to follow her. Joining the queue that had already formed at the self service cafeteria counter he indulged himself with two cups of coffee and a cholesterol-laden but enormously satisfying 'English breakfast'. Finally when there was no sign of his travelling companion returning he purchased a couple of newspapers and settled himself in one of the lounge areas.

With the crossing taking less than two hours it seemed to Anna that the time spent on deck under the blue skies of the channel passed pleasantly but all too swiftly. The fact that Martin Price seemed to breezily take her willingness to join his Sarony trip for granted, and the deliberately half baked manner in which they were travelling, irritated her beyond measure. She could put up with Rod McEwan's comments in the knowledge that they were designed to needle her given his dislike of Martin Price, but the fact that the remarks were proving uncomfortably close to the truth was not reassuring. Getting away into the fresh air was what she needed to restore her spirits, and she was used to spending time alone enjoying her own company. Looking out at the rippling water as the ferry stolidly churned its way towards France calmed her feelings although she would have been dismayed to learn that from then on her journey would take a sharp downhill turn.

It was as they were getting back into the Land Rover that the first incident occurred. The much admired Range Rover parked ahead of them was the conveyance of two couples who, according to a number of stickers applied to the rear window, were ardent supporters of Liverpool FC. This initial impression was confirmed by the noisy return of two men and two women in their late thirties and early forties. The men sported close cropped heads and at least one earring apiece. Various tattoos on arms protruding from short sleeved football shirts did nothing to dispel the maxim that men of a certain age should not dress as teenagers. They were however surpassed by their companions, who were also garbed in teenage style, with outfits that appeared to have been designed for women a size or two smaller than the wearers. As a result there were displayed a large number of bodily cracks and crevices that would have been far better hidden from public display. A rousing chorus of some indecipherable football chant accompanied them as they squeezed between the vehicles armed with clanking bags from the duty-free shop, and the slightly unsteady walk of the two women betrayed the fact that they had spent a large portion of the crossing as patrons of the ferry bar.

"Someone's had a good start to the day" commented Martin, and the words were no sooner out of his mouth than one of the women lurched against the front wing of the Land Rover and snagged her jeans on a slightly jagged seam of metal.

"Ooh bloody 'ell" she exclaimed as the material ripped an inch long hole on her hip.

Martin wound down his window "Are you all right?" he asked and was rewarded with a glare followed by "You wanna do something about this junk heap mate, bloody dangerous."

He ignored the comment and asked "You aren't hurt are you, not drawn blood has it?"

"No thanks to you mate, ruined my fucking jeans it has," came the unladylike retort."

He nodded and said "You could have been a bit more careful couldn't you?"

At this point the driver of the Range Rover walked back and pointed a threatening finger "And you'd better watch it pal, bloody Southerners. Go and buy yourself a decent set of wheels."

Anna saw Martin's hands tense on the steering wheel as he replied in a very steady almost soft voice "The car wasn't moving, your friend here walked into it. Not the other way round."

"Oh for God's sake let it go," muttered Anna.

At that point what looked like turning into a more unpleasant situation was interrupted, and then curtailed, by the loudspeaker announcing that all passengers were to board their vehicles and make ready to disembark. Car engines started, the Range Rover doors closed and the noise of the ramp being lowered drifted through the vehicle deck. Anna sat back and was relieved to see the cars ahead of them begin to move off as the already perceptibly warmer French air flooded into the car deck. As they pulled out of the dock area Martin said "I know a very nice little café on the outskirts and thought we could have lunch before heading South, is that OK?"

She nodded "That sounds nice, I could do with something to eat after the crossing, being out in the open air gives one a hunger."

"In that case you will like this place, they do some of the best sea food in the region. It's run by a couple of friends of mine. I always try and look in on them when I'm in Calais."

"Do you come over to France often?"

"Not as much as I'd like although now I don't have any major commitments at home I should be able to indulge myself a little more, and I've quite a few friends living here. I thought that a light lunch would tide us over for later. We could set off directly afterwards and get to Sarony approaching seven. We are expected at Auberge Fleurie and should be able to have a decent freshen up, dinner, and a good rest before our first site visit tomorrow. How does that sound?"

"You've got it all organised by the sound of it, I'll trust your judgement."

Lunch initially went very well although Anna was reluctant to exchange too much in the way of personal information, and so conversation had ground to a halt as they each silently sipped their coffee.

When mulling over her companion's character she decided that there was something about Martin Price that made her very wary of him. It wasn't mistrust exactly, nor was it concern for her personal well-being. Rod McEwan's suspicions had given her plenty of food for thought and she was resolved to treat Martin Price with cautious reserve. Unfortunately her general manner meant that this so called reserve could be interpreted as outright hostility, and her companion's response was to treat her in turn with a baffled politeness that destroyed any chance they may have had of developing a sociable relationship.

She looked sidelong at her companion as her thoughts explored the enigma that surrounded him. On the face of it he was a very relaxed easy going person, not particularly good looking but quite presentable to look at, and with a certain amount of personal charm that she may in a different situation have found attractive. What made her uneasy – yes that was the word – was that she had occasionally caught a glimpse of a different Martin Price when he crossed swords with someone. It seemed that there was an underlying hardness that lay beneath his placid good natured exterior. It didn't erupt into outright anger but, instead, manifested itself in an unyielding single mindedness that seemed prepared to brush any opposition to one side.

When they had encountered the football people on the car deck she had watched as the woman was talking to Price and noticed how he seemed to carefully switch on an air of relaxed geniality. Then as soon as the woman's male companion became involved she had watched the geniality slowly evaporate and felt a distinct tension begin to build up. It wasn't just something ethereal, but a definite physical tensing of his muscles and she had seen that despite no noticeable movement his hands had tightened their grip on the steering wheel. She was greatly relieved when the order to disembark had unexpectedly distracted all parties. Almost as if her mind was being read by some malevolent emissary of the Gods she looked up to see the familiar Range Rover with it's football stickers backing into one of the parking spaces opposite.

The café itself was situated in a small square with access from streets either side of the buildings opposite. It was set back from the kerbside behind a wide expanse of paving stones that afforded room for a number of tables and chairs to be positioned outside, although on Martin's advice they had chosen a table set back in the cool interior. Their arrival had been accompanied by much hearty backslapping and quick fire French from the elderly owner whose name Martin had informed her was Bertrand. His equally elderly wife Emilie was introduced to her when repeated shouted exhortations from Bertrand finally caused her to emerge from the depths of the kitchen.

"Marti, Marti" she had screeched as she engulfed Martin in her not inconsiderable bulk. She whispered something that made him laugh and stroked his face before suddenly noticing Anna's presence. With a "Pardon M'selle" she took a pace backwards and allowed the formal introductions to be made before scurrying back to her kingdom at the rear. Now, as sole remaining customers in the aftermath of an excellent lunch, and a glass of wine or two – or was it three? – Anna was mulling over the antipathy she felt for her companion as he sat with half closed eyes in the shadows to her left.

The Range Rover couples had made their way across the square and sat themselves down in the sunshine with much clattering of chairs and loud conversation. Watching from the interior Anna silently cursed the fates that had brought them to this peaceful spot.

The taller and more heavily tattooed of the men had attracted a dozing Bertrand's attention by leaning back in his chair, snapping his fingers and in the time honoured Neanderthal fashion adopted by the British in France calling loudly "Garcon, 'ay garcon." Bertrand having attended as requested was faced with a tattooed arm surmounted by four upright fingers and the words "Quatro beers pal". It then took a further exchange in broken English, although Anna realised that Bertrand understood the language perfectly well, for the tattooed one to explain that it was four large beers from the pump that were required and not "those poxy little bottles of gnat's piss that you Frenchies drink." This last comment was made against a background accompaniment of high pitched laughter from the females and the comment "Tell 'im 'Arry' from the second man in the group as Bertrand bustled off to get the drinks.

It occurred to Anna that all four of the party were a little the worse for wear, the women more so than the men, and having indulged during the ferry crossing had clearly been drinking elsewhere in Calais before deciding to disrupt this small enclave of tourist-free peace. She wished that she could be magically transported away from her country-folk to a distant desert island, but a glance at Martin revealed that apart from briefly flicking his eyes open, taking in their new visitors and then closing them again he was apparently unconcerned by the intrusion.

The talk at the table in front of the café became more raucous, and the language coarser, as the drinks were rapidly consumed. One of the women finally lurched to her feet and announced loudly that she needed to relieve herself, although using a blunter expression that brought forth further laughter and ribald comments from her companions. As she passed through to the toilets that were set beyond the bar, she noticed for the first time

Anna and Martin at their table, and cast a venomous look in their direction. Bertrand meanwhile was having some trouble with the pump behind the bar, and taking longer than his customers thought reasonable to deliver the next order of beers which brought forth a stream of foul language and for some obscure reason a football chant from the occupants of the outside table. Having completed her ablutions the blonde had managed to encase herself once more in the skin tight jeans and strutted, rather than walked, through the cafe before pausing alongside the seated Anna and standing theatrically, hand on hip, with the clear intention of resuming the earlier argument. The tear in her jeans was still plain and she looked first at Anna and then Martin, her mouth opened and instead of the expected torrent nothing came out. Anna turned in surprise to look at Price and saw that he was now sitting upright and staring with grave intensity directly into the other woman's eyes. His face was expressionless but at the same time it seemed to convey an ominous message. The blonde apparently thinking it wiser not to make her intended comment, closed her mouth and moved on but the delay had meant that Bertrand, having now finally produced four fresh glasses of beer, had exited the bar and was also heading towards the outside table only a couple of paces behind her.

"About bloody time" roared 'Arry.

Unaware of Bertrand's presence, and assuming the remark was addressed to her, the blonde stopped and shrieked "It's a lot quicker for you blokes to have a piss, so lay off."

Bertrand had meanwhile sidestepped the woman and was in the process of lowering the tray of drinks to the table when she moved to her right, knocking his arm and causing one of the beers to tip over and cascade it's contents onto the tray from which a good amount then splashed into the lap of the woman seated to his right. His apologies were drowned by the unlucky recipient's squeal of dismay and a torrent of abuse from 'Arry as both men leapt to their feet.

"Oh shit," muttered Anna as the pantomime unfolded in her full view.

Martin on the other hand remained unperturbed, and simply watched as Bertrand hastily mopped up, and carefully put the remaining glasses onto the table. The commotion appeared to be dying down as he first made as if to head back to the café with the empty glasses, and then turned back to the beer splattered woman and said something that caused her to shake her head and wave him away in an irritated fashion. It was then that 'Arry became more directly involved as he took a step forward, put a meaty hand on Bertrand's shoulder and gave him a hefty shove to encourage him to return to the café. Unfortunately the elderly proprietor's foot caught against the large handbag deposited by the blond woman on the ground near her chair, and he sprawled headlong.

For a man in his seventies such accidents are to be avoided and, as Anna half rose to her feet in consternation, Martin Price moved more swiftly from his chair than she would have thought possible. Within seconds he was helping the old man to his feet. Events then unfolded at a rapid pace. Anna had risen and moved around the table to see if she could be of help, although she was still unable to fathom how Price was able to move so swiftly from a sitting position. Meanwhile, Emilie emerged from the rear kitchen to see what all the noise was about. As Bertrand stood shakily dusting himself down Anna saw Martin say something to 'Arry, and whatever it was it caused the big man to take two steps forward with his fist upraised which put him between Martin Price and the Anna's line of vision.

It was only when she thought about it afterwards that Anna was able to view the rapid unfolding of the incident in its entirety, almost like a slow motion replay. With the broad back of the taller man obscuring Price from sight she saw the tattooed arm descend in a swinging right-hander. At first nothing seemed to happen and then, seconds after what should have been the sound of the blow striking her companion, there came the noise of a sharp crack that caused all other sound from the front table to abruptly cease. Moving forwards she saw 'Arry suddenly stiffen and he seemed to draw himself up to beyond his normal height of six feet two inches before falling forward across the circular metal table as Martin stepped adroitly to one side. Unable to resist 'Arry's weight and impetus the table tipped sideways scattering glasses and beer in all directions. The women screamed, and the unconscious form of the big Liverpudlian absorbed several unpleasantly shaped shards of broken glass before coming to rest amidst the debris that now littered the pavement. By this time Anna had arrived at the scene and, looking down, was horrified to see that hitting the table had caused 'Arry to twist in his headlong descent and come to rest face upwards displaying a bloody mess of a nose from which blood now pumped forth in alarming quantities.

"You've bloody killed 'Arry" screeched the blonde as she dropped to her knees beside the spread-eagled form.

Anna switched her gaze to Price and was shocked to observe the look of cold detachment registered on his face as he said "Turn him on his side so he doesn't choke. He'll need some medical assistance to re-set his nose."

"You fucking bastard" the words came not from one of the women, but from the other man who although initially frozen with indecision had suddenly come to life. Stooping to grab the jagged lower half of a beer glass he lunged at Price from the side. For the second time in a few minutes it seemed to Anna that time was somehow distorted as without appearing to look, her companion turned his upper body slightly and let the lethal piece of glassware pass his nose by no more than half an inch. His right hand fastened on the outstretched wrist of his assailant, jerked it expertly downwards and then behind the man's back. An upward thrust produced a scream of pain, and the second bone cracking noise of the afternoon. His left hand had at the same time grabbed a handful of hair and the man found himself forced to his knees, whereupon Martin's right knee was planted with a sickening crunch in his face. More blood, more screeching, and 'Arry's friend was left kneeling semi conscious amidst blood and vomit as his distraught partner burst into tears.

From the moment the beer was spilt to the moment Martin Price put his arm around Bertrand's shoulders and guided him back to the bar, less than three minutes had elapsed. Anna bent to help the blonde woman who was in the process of turning her incoherently groaning husband onto his side and was rewarded with a "Piss off" for her trouble. She turned to see the second man still kneeling in an uncomprehending daze amidst the carnage, as his woman vainly tried to help him to his feet. Feeling bemused by the lightning fast turn of events, and not a little sickened by the violent outcome, she headed back to the bar as Price handed Bertrand a glass of brandy, and patted him on the shoulder. Emilie had now joined the Range Rover casualties and was talking animatedly on a mobile phone. Price said something further to Bertrand who nodded and waved him away. He turned, intercepted her as she had almost reached the café entrance and said "Come on, no point in hanging around here."

She looked at him aghast "Wha-what do you mean? We can't just leave. What about them?" she waved a hand at the group behind her.

"Bertrand and Emilie will deal with that. Come on, if we are here when the emergency services turn up we will never get on the road this side of Christmas."

Her outrage expanded "You can't just walk away Martin."

He let go the elbow that he had grabbed to steer her towards the old Land Rover and replied in a very quiet level tone "I can and I am. If you want to stay here, be my guest, but as I said, Bertrand and Emilie will deal with the mess, and I am driving to Sarony."

As they drove out onto the main road leading South the sound of sirens could clearly be heard in the distance behind them.

"They are looking for us" muttered Anna

"No" came the response "they won't come after us."

"You could have killed that big fellow"

His reply shook her "I could have killed them both but I didn't."

"Did you deliberately provoke that man? I saw you say something to him."

"I told him to pick on someone his own size."

"Oh very smart, just the thing to cool the situation down," she said sarcastically before lapsing into sullen silence. Nothing more was said for the next one hundred and fifty miles until the brooding became too much for her to bear.

"Don't you care how badly hurt they are?" She suddenly snapped as the Land Rover changed lanes to follow the Lyon signs.

Perhaps it was the long period of silence and her sudden return to the attack that did it, but for the first time she saw him display true anger as he replied.

"I know how badly hurt they are, and I hope it's enough to stop them doing the same thing again. Bertrand received a medal for outstanding bravery during the Algerian conflict from De Gaulle himself. He carried a wounded comrade to safety under intense fire, and I'm not going to stand by and see him, in his seventies, get pushed around by something that's crawled out from under a rock. He's my friend and whatever some opinionated, snooty, pain in the arse, seen nothing and done less, academic thinks is of no interest to me. Bertrand and Emilie will deal with the police, there never was an old Land Rover near the cafe, they don't know any English couple, it was all the usual English hooligans."

She sat stunned into silence by the vehemence of his tirade and realised that for the first time he had actually lashed out at her on a personal level. There followed another long acrimonious period of Arctic calm during which the Land Rover turned onto one of the Route National roads and then again onto a D road.

The traffic had lessened as they progressed and the road was almost deserted. Anna sat smouldering with her thoughts until the sound of motorcycle engines caused her to look with apprehension in the wing mirror. She winced involuntarily as instead of the expected police presence three large and very expensive looking machines, of the kind often seen in American films, flashed past very close to the passenger side and cut in dangerously sharply in front of the Land Rover. She thrust her hands out in front of her as incredibly Price made no attempt to moderate his speed and the bikes were forced to edge faster to avoid the collision their actions had invited. For several hundred yards they travelled at high speed worryingly close to the bikes strung three abreast ahead of them, and each time the bikers began to reduce their speed the front bumper of the Land Rover crept inexorably towards their rear wheels as Price made it abundantly clear that he would have no hesitation in driving straight through them rather than slow down. Angry looks were thrown over the shoulders of the leather jacketed riders, but the attempted intimidation had no affect and finally the rider of the central machine turned, made the internationally recognised one finger gesture and all three accelerated away and were soon only specks in the distance.

Near to tears from a combination of anger and fear Anna shakily asked "Supposing they had suddenly braked?"

"They wouldn't" came the assured reply "They may be idiots but they are not entirely stupid. Playing chicken is the oldest trick in the book and if I'd slowed they would then have gone slower still, and so on. Finally I would have had to stop and they would most likely have tried to rob us. Now our turn for Sarony is coming up, see that white signpost up ahead?"

He began to slow down and was almost at the point of turning off when she said "Stop the car Martin, I'm getting out".

Thinking she was feeling unwell he made the turn and came to a halt a few yards into the narrow side road that wound its way through the fir trees lining each side. To his surprise she threw open her door, hopped nimbly out and said "I've had enough, I'm getting my case and going back."

"Don't be daft," he called as she made her way to the rear, how are you going to get back from here? Come into Sarony and take some time to cool down. If you still want to return we can get a cab number from the auberge."

"I don't want any more so-called help from you, I've figured out your little game and I'm going to beg a lift from the next car that comes along. I've got my mobile if I need to make other arrangements. Now bugger off to Sarony and find someone else to beat up."

Martin stared at the girl for a short time before shrugging and saying "Sarony is about seven miles down this road, if you change your mind phone me and I'll come out to get you."

She didn't answer, choosing instead to walk back towards the D road with the intention of waiting for a passing car. The comment about using her mobile was largely bravado as she had chosen German as her foreign language at school and had very little in the way of French vocabulary. As she stomped towards the road entrance the trundling noise made by the little plastic suitcase wheels was drowned by the sound of the Land Rover engine as it pulled away, and headed off in the opposite direction.

Chapter 7 - The Forest

Fifty minutes later she was standing miserably at the same spot without having seen a single vehicle come past from either direction. The light was a little less clear and the sun was now noticeably lower than when she had left the Land Rover. The tall trees of the pine forest cast long shadows despite it still being several hours before sunset and, as she was pondering whether it was worth walking back along the D road in the hope of perhaps striking a more frequented route, she heard a familiar noise in the distance. An irrational panic gripped her as the sound grew in intensity. Grabbing the handle of the suitcase she struggled through the grassy undergrowth into the line of fir trees. Without quite knowing why she urgently pumped her long legs in awkward frantic strides, breathlessly towing the suitcase as it bounced and hopped over roots and grassy tufts as the rucksack thumped against her back. The effort, and her own fear, caused her to miss the upraised root; tripping headlong she sprawled full length in the dusty smelly soil between the trees. It was a heavy tumble and both knees of her jeans were torn with the skin beneath becoming grazed and in one case oozing blood.

The roar of motorcycle engines reached a crescendo as the three riders drew to a halt at the very spot she had so recently vacated. She quietly inched herself around on the ground and looked towards the road. Voices drifted on the evening air as one of the leather jacketed figures began to slowly amble in her direction. She was sure it was the same trio that had tried to intimidate them earlier that afternoon and, as she held her breath, she wished she had taken up the offer to phone from the village.

The figure stopped and fumbled with the front of his jeans. She closed her eyes, kept perfectly still, and listened to the sound of running water splashing into the undergrowth only a matter of yards away. The man's two companions had stayed with their machines, legs straddled and feet planted securely on the road surface as he relieved himself. A brief comment was flung out as he zipped up his jeans and strolled back to the road causing him to laugh, and make an indecipherable riposte. She lay in abject discomfort waiting for them to move on but was forced to endure a further ten minutes as they took the opportunity for a smoke. It seemed more like ten years to Anna as she lay with her face pressed against the dank earth, but finally, cigarettes consumed, they resumed their journey. Within seconds all three had roared away from the roadside and their engine noises were only a fast fading echo in the stillness of the forest. She sat up, brushed the dust and twigs that clung to her clothing and gingerly rose to her feet.

It seemed that almost every year a newspaper story was published recounting in sensational terms how tourists becoming lost in rural France had fallen prey to thieves and murderers. She had no wish to discover what might befall a foreign woman like herself who encountered three Hells Angels out in the wilds of a French forest and made the decision to swallow her pride. Her hand fished in her rucksack for the mobile phone, gratefully clutched the protective leather case then, as the reassuring screen lit up, it just as swiftly blinked out. With a sick feeling in the pit of her stomach she realised that it was out of charge and the only option was to walk. Abandoning her suitcase she made her way back out of the trees and onto the side road. Noticing for the first time a small stone shrine on the roadside opposite, she made a mental note to use it as an additional landmark to help locate her suitcase the following day.

Seven miles was what Martin Price had said – or did he mean kilometres? A hopeful thought, but after being acquainted with him for a even a short time she knew that he never said what he didn't mean. So it was going to be a seven mile walk in soft casual shoes that, while reasonably well made, were certainly never intended to be used over any distance as walking shoes. In a determined frame of mind she set off at a good enough pace and cursed the shadows cast by the fir trees lining the road which made the light not only dimmer than normal for that time of the evening, but also gave a sinister feel to her solitary progress towards Sarony. To town dwellers it is rarely appreciated just how much noise actually occurs in a supposedly peaceful and deserted rural setting, and so initially her nerves became even more taut whenever a pine cone bumped and bounced it's way downwards, or a squirrel or bird blundered through it's leafy habitat heedless of the affect on the hurrying human below. Her imagination added urgency to her walking pace as thoughts of rape and murder in a lonely spot crowded her mind. If those men came back and stumbled upon her she could be killed, her body thrown in amongst the trees and it would be years before she was discovered. Damn Martin Price, if he wasn't such a bloody insufferable know-all she wouldn't be in this predicament.

As time passed, the road surface began to show signs of breaking up in large patches as nature successfully conducted its unrelenting war of attrition against the man-made incursions into its domain. One of Anna's shoes began to split and after half an hour had rubbed a sore spot on the outside of her little toe. All the time she kept alert for the sound of motorcycle engines and regularly checked her watch to try and judge her progress. She had been walking for an hour when her shoe finally gave way altogether and she hurled both items of footwear into the trees. The heavy rucksack was chafing her shoulders and despite the lack of warming sunshine she was sweating with the exertion of trying to maintain a brisk pace.

Although she was fortunate to encounter few sharp objects on her journey those occasional pointed stones or holes in the tarmac did hurt her feet and in some instances broke the skin. Her strides became shorter and she seemed to be forever hitching the rucksack into a more comfortable position. Her rate of progress had slowed partly due to the lack of footwear and also to the fact that she was simply beginning to tire. On average a brisk walking speed is judged to be four miles per hour but she realised after an hour that her optimistic hope that she could reach journey's end in ninety minutes would prove woefully inaccurate.

Time passed as Anna toiled onwards. If this was England, she thought, there would have been a small country pub, or at the very least the occasional car, but here in France it was if the entire country had decided to retire early for the night. It was quite incredible, she thought bitterly, that she could walk for mile after mile and encounter not a solitary fellow member of the human race.

The shadows were lengthening as a fox broke cover and dashed across the road a few yards ahead, its sudden appearance jolting her mind back to a more alert state. It was all very well hoping to meet another person on this damned road, but who was to say that it would be a knight in shining armour? She smiled grimly at the picture that popped into her mind of a medieval figure on horseback. Chretien de Sarony had been a knight in shining armour, and it was due to him and Mr Martin-bloody-know-it-all-Price that she was tramping along in the middle of nowhere with bleeding feet, aching shoulders and shredded nerves. The self pity finally broke her spirit and she came to an abrupt halt, sat down in the middle of the road and burst into tears.

The fox, on it's way back to it's lair, went unnoticed even though it stopped and stared at the strange creature with grazed knees that rocked backwards and forwards whilst emitting snuffling, wailing sounds. Eventually Anna artistically applied streaks of dirt across her face as she wiped the tears away and struggled to her feet. Despite it's valuable cargo she was even considering ditching the rucksack when she caught the first glimpse of a light ahead piercing the gathering gloom. It was almost three hours since she had first fled from the place where the motorcycle trio had halted, and although she tried to pick up the pace, her painful feet refused to respond. It was in a demoralised and exhausted condition that Anna Freemont trudged out of the gloomy confines of the pine forest and along the road that lead through the small village of Sarony.

Chapter 8 - Monique

Sarony was a typical French village laying within many square miles of farmland punctuated by pine forests. The majority of its buildings lined the road along which Anna now despondently limped on bare, damaged feet, and ahead of her on the left hand side she could see a break in the buildings that was picked out by red white and blue coloured lights. As she drew closer the lights proved to mark out an open air patio on which a number of tables were set. Beyond the patio lay a two story building from which a projecting sign proclaimed 'Auberge Fleurie' and, further on again, could be seen a small arched entrance through which a narrow driveway led to a courtyard parking area.

Thirsty, sweaty, tired, and feeling decidedly tearful, Anna nonetheless felt enormously relieved that her long and upsetting day of travel was now coming to an end. A number of the patio tables were occupied and the sound of cutlery being wielded with Gallic enthusiasm combined with the hum of conversation became louder as she neared her destination. The sound of a woman's laughter drifted out on the evening air. In the gathering gloom, seated at a table nearest the road, she enviously noticed a young woman smiling and wildly waving a glass of wine in one hand. Her companion sat facing away from Anna and chuckled before adding something in a softer tone that caused the woman to throw back her head and let forth a further peal of attractive musical merriment. As she began to walk wearily past on her way

80

towards the entrance, the woman said something to her companion. He casually glanced around, stiffened, and then jumped to his feet saying "Anna, good grief what on earth are you doing here? Hang on, I'll come through and get you." He strode across the patio, through a side door into the building before reappearing seconds later on the roadside.

"Christ you look dreadful" was his next remark which produced a tired "Thanks" as she let him guide her through the auberge entrance and, via a busy bar area, out onto the patio. He led her across to the table by the roadside at which a solitary female figure now sat, said something in rapid French, and the woman immediately got to her feet and hurried past them back into the bar.

"Sit down Anna, you look done in, how the devil have you got into this state? Look, let me take the damned rucksack, and why aren't you wearing shoes?" Before she had a chance to respond, his erstwhile table companion reappeared clutching a bottle of red wine, a carafe of water, and some additional glasses which she set expertly on the table. The two fresh glasses were filled with wine and water and pushed before Anna with the words

"Drink Cherie, food will be a little while yet – we were not expecting you, I am Monique." The speaker turned to Martin and continued with "Marti, is this 'er, you were telling me about?"

He responded with "Monique, allow me to introduce Anna Freemont, and Anna may I have the pleasure of

81

acquainting you with one of my very best friends M'selle Monique Lascelles."

Anna, who had consumed most of the glass of water and moved on to sample the fortifying qualities of the wine, was forced to reluctantly put down her glass and offer a weak "Hello Monique," as she held out her rather grubby hand. At the same time she felt a sinking feeling in her stomach that owed nothing to the wine, but resulted from her swift appraisal of the French woman.

She was everything a British person expected of a female from 'La Belle France.' Her excellent figure was accentuated by a close fitting sweater. This surmounted a well cut pleated skirt that was short enough to attract admiring glances for the shapely legs and elegant feet tucked into high heeled shoes. Black hair tied back in a shiny exuberant pony tail and a very pretty face with dark eyes and a ready smile completed the picture, and Anna briefly hated her.

But only briefly, because Monique topped up her wine glass and rising to her feet reached out to take her hand whilst addressing Martin with the words "This one cannot eat with us in this state Marti, go and tell Thierry that we will have dinner in 'arf an hour, and to ensure there is more than enough for three. I am taking Anna upstairs with me."

The fact that Monique dished out her orders with such assurance surprised Anna almost as much as the way Martin Price headed obediently in the direction of the bar. As he did so she felt compelled to rise by the insistent hold Monique had of her hand, and allowed herself to be towed towards the door through which Price had just disappeared. "Come, come Cherie, you will soon feel better and look beautiful again" purred Monique. They eased their way through the crowded bar with the French woman exchanging comments with some of the patrons, who were clearly intrigued by the tall scruffy blonde.

Anna followed Monique up a narrow stairway to the first floor and along a passageway punctuated by eight doors, one of which provided entry to Monique's private quarters, with the others providing access to the rooms available for paying guests. She was swept into a small living room and on into a beautifully decorated bedroom. Monique finally released her hand, whirled to face her and rapped out the single word "Strip" although it came out as 'Streep'.

"What?" Anna asked, then understood as Monique flung open a door to reveal an en-suite bathroom.

"I will give you clean clothes, give me these." She gestured impatiently. "Allez Cherie. I want my dinner."

She self consciously undressed before Monique's critical gaze and watched as her discarded bra was scooped up and closely examined before again being imperiously waved towards the bathroom accompanied by the exhortation to "Use anything but quick, quick."

It was the best shower she had ever had and in twenty minutes she was combing her damp hair into straight untangled lengths before stepping back into the bedroom.

She was immediately confronted by Monique holding out a beautiful, white lace adorned bra in one hand, and a matching pair of panties in the other. She reached out to take the offerings and her covering towel dropped to the floor causing Monique to snatch back the bra, examine it closely then make a circle in the air with her forefinger and say "Around."

Anna did a prompt about face and then gasped with surprise and embarrassment as Monique manoeuvred her expertly into the bra and then proceeded to grasp both her breasts and jiggle them into a more comfortable position before muttering "Bon" followed by "Allez Cherie, allez."

She slipped on the panties and turned to find Monique holding out a simple yellow summer dress and noticed a similar coloured cardigan laying on the double bed. Barely half an hour had passed by the time she eased her tender feet into a pair of unflattering, but mercifully comfortable, casual shoes and stood before Monique's unwavering gaze.

"It is ok. You are not quite the same shape up here as me," she pronounced, patting her own generous bust, "but not bad. Now let us eat Cherie." Brushing aside Anna's thanks Monique led the way back to the ground floor and out to where Martin Price sat with his feet resting on a vacant chair nursing a full glass of wine, having clearly replenished it from the second bottle that had magically appeared on the table. Looking for all the world as if he owned the place he grinned as they approached and said

"My word, what a transformation, the local wine obviously agrees with you."

It was a feeble attempt at humour that was deservedly ignored by Anna as she thankfully lowered herself onto a chair. Barely had her glass been refilled than a sturdy individual, who was clearly the 'Thierry' Monique had referred to earlier, bustled up to them and began to unload cutlery, plates, and covered pots from a huge tray. The resulting steaming dishes that were distributed smelt to Anna like the most appetizing food she had ever encountered, and she launched into it in a most unrefined manner.

It was a strange meal, with Martin and Monique valiantly attempting to involve Anna in the conversation, while for her part she was mainly concerned with assuaging the hunger that her walk and shower had produced. In between mouthfuls she briefly described the hours she had spent since deciding to turn back, but her conversation was stilted through tiredness. Faced with her increasingly monosyllabic responses and frequent lapses into silence, Martin and Monique switched into French and conversed between themselves as she miserably worked off her appetite.

Part of the reason for her mood was that she didn't actually know why she felt so unhappy. Earlier in the day it had been anger at what she perceived to be Price's high handed – not to say aggressive – behaviour. On further reflection she wondered whether it was the accumulation of events scattered throughout the day that were now rounded off by her companions being considerate towards her in such a studied fashion.

That was another thing – why did he always act so good naturedly, and exactly what sort of terms was he on with the attractive buxom French girl who seemed to hang on his every word? She sullenly observed the two of them totally at ease with one another, breaking into an occasional chuckle. Monique, eyes twinkling as she reached across and patted Martin's hand, he with a laid back, almost mischievous, tone to his voice as he clearly made gentle fun of something Monique had said. Like lovers, thought Anna, and they obviously knew each other well as this day's booking was so evidently not their first encounter.

At that moment Price said something that made Monique almost choke on her wine as she shrieked with laughter and an irritated Anna made up her mind to end the torture and turn in for the night. She was too slow however as Monique tottered to her feet with her body still racked by the humour and, switching to English, said, "I must help Thierry clear the bar, and then I am going to bed. Anna, your room is, um, number 6, pick up the key from behind the bar when you go up, Marti will show you. Marti, you are ....., well I do not know the English word but I will show you instead," and to Anna's astonishment she walked around the table and planted a lingering kiss on his lips before heading for the bar.

Despite having done nothing to resist Monique's demonstration of affection, Price looked apologetically at Anna and said "I'm sorry about that Anna, Monique is very, well, French I suppose, and we have known each other for some years."

She was about to respond with something on lines of 'don't mind me, I'm going home tomorrow' when the barb died in her throat as he added,

"Look, we seem to have got off to a very bad start to say the least, and you were clearly far more upset by today's events than I appreciated. I am of course responsible for some of the upsets since we first met, but not all, and I'm bemused at the fact that you want to go back to Grantfield because you think I am somehow up to something. Why don't we both sleep on it tonight, and then have a proper discussion tomorrow at breakfast? I'll ask Monique to leave us alone so that we can speak frankly."

She looked at him, saw that there was no hint of anything other than concern in his eyes, nodded, finished the dregs of her coffee and said "Yes, that would be sensible wouldn't it," but couldn't resist adding "I'll need to have my case retrieved whatever the outcome."

Why wasn't she surprised when he said "Don't worry, Thierry is going to nip out first thing tomorrow and pick it up. It shouldn't take him long from the description you gave. Monique told me she would arrange it and also told me to say that you would find another change of clothes in your bedroom for the morning. Now I don't know about you, but it's been a long day and I think I'm about ready to turn in."

He retrieved both their keys and followed Anna up the stairs to the first floor corridor. To her surprise Price held out his hand and said "Well goodnight Anna. Sleep well."

Taken aback by the warm smile and gentle words she also smiled, shook his hand and replied,

"Thank you Martin, you too."

Anna's room was the typical, slightly eccentric offering of a French country inn, with furnishings a little shabby, but everything spotlessly clean, and true to her word Monique had provided a simple skirt, blouse and underclothes, no doubt from her own resources. One of the few useful items contained in her rucksack was a toilet bag and Anna eagerly seized her toothpaste and brush to banish the aftermath of the recent meal. When she went to check the time she realised with annoyance that she had left her wristwatch in Monique's bathroom and stood in her underwear for a moment before deciding that, as she had seen no evidence of any other overnight guests, it would be safe to scamper the few yards along to Monique's quarters.

She knocked gently on the door before remembering that if Monique was not in the outer room she would be unlikely to hear the cautious tapping. Carefully she turned the handle and to her relief the door opened into the living room that, although unlit, revealed a light shining from beneath the bedroom door on the far side. This time she knocked a little more firmly, called the occupant's name, and was gratified when the voice responded "Entree Cherie, come, come". On entering it was clear that Monique had been reading as she lay down a magazine and, heedless of her now exposed breasts as she leaned sideways, smilingly picked up Anna's watch from her bedside cabinet saying "I found it by the shower." Anna gratefully thanked her and was about to retrace her steps when Monique said "You must not make a silly mistake Cherie."

"What do you mean?"

"I mean that you must not throw away something very important, something I know I can never have."

It was noticeable that Monique's use of English became formal, almost stilted when imparting some serious information, but descended into a one word autocratic style with dropped aitches when agitated.

"You seem to have quite a lot already" replied a mystified Anna gesturing to her surroundings.

Monique frowned then flicked back the sheets and said "We cannot speak like this Cherie and you will get cold. Get in next to me and we will talk about why you are so unhappy, allez vous."

For some reason her words brought tears to Anna's eyes and she eased herself beneath the sheets. Monique turned towards her, slid her right arm around her shoulders and drew her against her warm body with the words "Listen to my words Cherie" and her left hand gently stroked Anna's right arm as the tears rolled slowly down the blonde girl's cheeks.

"You say I seem to have a lot, but what you see here is only half mine, I share it with Marti. So I have half of all of this, but nothing of what I have always most desired."

"I-I'm not sure I understand" whispered Anna.

This provoked a sigh from her companion who tightened her embrace and said "I will explain some but not all, because all would be too much, and not the correct way to go. I grew up in another village close to Sarony, but things were not good and I became, how do you say it, a tart? That was what I was when I met Marti."

Her words caused Anna to stiffen as she asked "You mean he was a customer, er client?"

"Ha, no Cherie no. But don't get me wrong, we have had our moments as you English say. But no, Marti is the reason I now have what I have. I was working for a man who was not kind and one day he was giving me a beating by the roadside where I had sat for hours on my little chair without earning, and Marti happened to see us. I was very afraid when he beat the man who was meant to be my protector" – she laughed in derision at the description- "but then he made me come to Sarony, here to Auberge Fleurie, and told me I was to work as a barmaid and nothing else. I could live here and my food was all provided. The small wages were just for me, and whatever extra the customers gave me if they were happy, but not, you must understand Cherie, as a tart. He told me I was to stop selling myself."

"What happened?" asked Anna, now helplessly caught up in Monique's tale. "How did you manage to buy a share of this auberge?"

"Well I did not really do so Cherie. Old Henri who ran this place wanted to retire and when he left Marti asked me to run it instead – he already owned it of course, and then after a few months he told me he wanted to give me a half so that I would have somewhere to belong, and he would have someone he could trust to look after the property – it is quite old you see."

"I don't understand Monique what it is that you cannot have – you seem to have a good life now."

"Cherie you are blind, not foolish, but blind. I cannot have the thing I most desire because Marti does not love me. At least, not in the way I love him."

"Oh God."

"God will not help Cherie, I am not unhappy, and in Marti I still have a friend that some people can only hope for."

"And a lover?"

"In the past it has happened when one of us needed love, yes. But never when Marti has had a woman he is attached to, and not now for a long time."

"What about his mother Monique, didn't he need love when she was dying?"

For the first time Anna felt and heard anger from Monique as the woman took hold of her jaw between thumb and forefinger and turned her head so that she was forced to look directly into the blazing eyes.

"Did he run to me like, like a little boy you mean? What is the matter with you Cherie, do you understand nothing? Do you think he would want that sort of love from me when he was caring for his dying maman?"

"N-no Monique, I don't know anything about Martin and his mother. We are only working partners, not even friends. That is why I can't believe that you think I should have feelings for Martin."

"You are blind Cherie" said Monique as the anger dissolved as fast as it had flared, and she stroked the blonde hair.

It was five o'clock in the morning when Anna slipped from Monique's bed and padded quietly back to her own. She lay for an hour awake and troubled before showering and readying herself for the encounter with Martin Price at breakfast. Noises began to filter up from the ground floor and when she finally plucked up the courage to negotiate the bar she found it unoccupied and on stepping onto the patio discovered him already sitting at the same table as before, studying a newspaper as he consumed his first coffee of the morning.

Chapter 9 - Breakfast

"'Morning" he smiled as he looked up and pushed a cup towards her. "Coffee, and whatever else you would like as soon as Thierry returns, hopefully with your case. How was your night?"

She shifted uncomfortably, avoided direct eye contact and mumbled "Fine thanks" as she poured her coffee.

"Think you might be interested in this." He said as he passed the paper to her, but she waved it away saying.

"My French is non-existent Martin. What is it about?"

"Oh, it just says that following a disturbance between rival football fans at a café in Calais yesterday, four Brits have been packed off back home with French police declining to prefer charges."

"Ah, so round one to you then."

"Are we in a competition?"

"Aren't we?"

"Perhaps you are right and you should take a cab back home" he said.

The sudden volte face took her breath away, and for the first time she tried to build a bridge. "I'm sorry, I seem to have misread your intention." She stammered.

"I was simply trying to reassure you Anna, that there would be no repercussions. I can't help being right, and as we did intend to talk things through I'd like to ask you something if I may?"

She nodded feeling a little numbed by his suddenly excessively polite tone. This bloody man Price was......she mentally slapped herself down. Get a grip for God's sake, his name is Martin, the French all seem to like him and call him Marti. The couple in Calais dote on him, Monique worships the ground he walks on. They can't all be wrong. Stop thinking negatively, his name is Martin. With difficulty she pulled her thoughts back into real time as he spoke.

"Well, bearing in mind I said nothing when that drunken old bag tore her jeans on the Land Rover, and at the café that clown began to bully an elderly friend of mine, not to mention his buddy trying to glass me, I'd be grateful if you would tell me why you consider me to be the bad guy in all this?

"I think you enjoyed hurting them, and I think that on the ferry you were hoping that the jeans incident would turn into something more belligerent."

She stared defiantly at him as he leaned back, arms folded across his chest and said, quite softly, without any hint of anger in his voice.

"Let's keep to the facts shall we? I said and did precisely nothing inflammatory on the ferry so unless you have become adept at reading my mind you have no foundation for saying that I wanted to escalate the matter. What you saw was me considering what the options would be if things did take a turn for the worse. At the café I dealt with a nasty position using minimum force to disable two opponents, one of whom had armed himself."

"Minimum force? OK, I grant you that you took on two bigger stronger drunks, but that's what they were Martin, drunks."

"So what should I have done? Tried to reason with them? Have you ever tried to reason with drunks while they play the hard man in front of their women? I won't deny that I have no regrets at taking them out, but enjoyment no, you've misread me completely."

"So it was necessary to smash your knee into that man's face after you had broken his arm was it?" Her voice had risen despite her effort to control the anger she felt at his careless attitude. But he came back at her just as calm as before and just as relentlessly.

"Yes absolutely, he had used a weapon, I broke his arm so he would drop the glass, and I smashed his nose so that next time he's in a fight he may think twice about arming himself. Look Anna, I don't go looking for trouble and, apart from the incident with the beer when we first met I don't usually lash out without good reason. For what it's worth I do regret soaking your Mr McEwan, if that's what you want to hear."

"He's not *my* Mr McEwan" she flared.

"Well you live with him, you work with him, and even when I asked to speak to you, guess who popped up? He's certainly not *my* Mr McEwan."

"It was you who chucked beer over him, was he supposed to be grateful?"

"OK, OK, but he was being a nuisance, as good as told me I was dishonest, and his supercilious interference was threatening to throw my afternoon schedule out. I needed to attend to mum and my irritation got the better of me, but you can't equate that with the way I dealt with those idiots at the café. It was what I was trained to do, and it has stood me in good stead over the years."

"*Trained* to do?"

"Yes, in the army, I spent a good time in uniform until mum was diagnosed with cancer."

"What regiment were you in?"

"I was in an infantry regiment, but I was well trained and I judged it the appropriate response yesterday to act as I did. Well, well, look who's come to say hello."

He had turned towards the roadside as a police car pulled in and a stern face looked out. The driver said something to his uniformed companion, alighted from the car and walked through the bar and out onto the patio. All six feet four inches headed purposefully for their table. Martin rose to his feet and for a moment Anna thought the unthinkable before the policeman's faced cracked into a welcoming smile and the two men threw their arms around each other. Naturally what followed was all in bloody French, but Anna thought she caught the words 'maman' and 'morte' uttered in a sorrowful tone before she heard Martin refer to 'M'selle Anna Freemont' and found herself confronted by the elegant newcomer.

"Anna Freemont, allow me to introduce Inspector Jean-Paul Ricard."

"Enchante M'selle" he announced taking her hand and proceeding to say in excellent English "I hope Marti (why do all the French call him Marti?) is looking after you and that the Coubert gang did not alarm you too much yesterday?"

"Actually Jean-Paul, the whole visit to Sarony has not been good for M'selle," interrupted Martin, "and I wonder if you would be able to give her a lift over to Belancourt station when you pass back though the village?"

"Ah so?" John-Paul's eyebrows twitched upwards. Anna blushed and contradicted Martin with a firm "I did intend to leave Monsieur, but I have changed my mind and I will be staying after all. We are here to work."

The eyebrows twitched again and beneath them the policeman's eyes flicked sideways to Martin, then back to Anna as he said. "That is good M'selle, I am sure you will enjoy Sarony, but excusez moi." The eyes left her "Marti, un moment." He drew Martin to one side and they again switched into French before reaching some sort of agreement with Jean-Paul murmuring "D'accord" before offering Anna a smile and "Au revoir M'selle, bon chance" and striding back to his car.

As the police car drew away, Anna turned to Martin and asked "What was all that about, and what is the Coubert gang when it's at home?"

Martin indicated their table and they resumed their seats. "Yes, well, unfortunately the Coubert gang are at home, and we were briefly acquainted with them yesterday."

"You mean the Hells Angels?"

"They're not real Hells Angels, just petty criminals and yobs who like to ride around looking tough. "I had a bit of a run in with their uncle a few years ago, and as a result we don't get on particularly well."

"That's why you wouldn't slow down yesterday isn't it."

"What I said was true – petty criminals. Stopping and robbing tourists, that sort of thing. I don't think they recognised me, and I had you with me so stopping would not have been a good move."

"What if they had recognised you Martin?"

He shrugged "I would have had to deal with it, but they didn't, so that's entirely academic. At least you took the right decision to stay out of their way when you almost bumped into them again."

"And Jean-Paul was warning you about them?"

"Sort of, he was telling me that they were around and, well, he asked me to avoid any trouble."

"Because of the incident with their uncle?"

"Yes, broadly speaking. More coffee? Ah, I see that Thierry has retrieved your case and is bringing over what looks like a good supply of croissants."

She allowed the conversation to drift away from the Coubert gang but couldn't shake off the feeling that there was something Martin wasn't telling her. They were almost immediately joined by Monique, and when Anna heard Jean-Paul's name mentioned, she noticed Monique nod very positively at something Martin both said and emphasised with an admonishing forefinger. He then turned to her and said in English "So you are staying after all?"

"Yes, and next time I'd prefer it if you let *me* make the announcements regarding my intentions. Let's get to work shall we, how do you suggest we proceed?"

Monique rose and said "Bon, Cherie," and stroked Anna's hair "I also have work, shall I hold a table for you this evening Marti?"

"Please, Monique" he answered. "I think Anna, that we should head for Chateau Sarony, it's only a few minutes drive and we can start our research."

They also rose and he motioned her to precede him as he said, "I will clue you in on what I know so far about Chretien de Sarony and his supposed treasure as we go."

The Land Rover was parked in the courtyard to the side of the auberge and as the engine started Anna said "You must know the owner pretty well Martin if you can just pitch up without phoning ahead, or have you already phoned?"

He didn't answer directly but instead said "Yes, we are well acquainted," and easing the Land Rover out through the small archway, turned left onto the road.

Chapter 10 - Chateau Sarony

"Do you know anything about the action that supposedly gave rise to the Sarony treasure?" he asked as they headed south.

"Only that it was a sort of side action compared to the Battle of Campomorto, and just happened to pay off big time due to the treasury of an Italian duke being held there."

"That's right, the short siege of Frosinone itself is notable for the fact that it first brought Chretien de Sarony to the attention of history. It wasn't a castle in the true sense of the word. It didn't possess a moat, but it was situated on top of high ground and could command the immediate area. It could more accurately be described as a garrisoned strongpoint and was extremely well provisioned and fortified. It even had its own well to supply fresh water. With it's garrison it was far too dangerous to leave untaken as it could also serve as a rallying point for other enemy troops who might otherwise simply desert.

An all out siege was not really much of an option for Chretien because it would take time, and mean he had to keep his troops in the field, living off the land while the garrison was tucked up in it's nice cosy fortress. So like any good commander he resorted to subterfuge in the form of bribery and corruption. He gained access to the fortress by the simple ruse of bribing one of the garrison to lower a rope from the wall and climb down to receive some gold in exchange for handing his clothing over and disappearing into the night. Chretien put on the disguise, climbed the rope, cut it loose and carefully made his way to the gatehouse where he killed the two guards.

Under cover of darkness a picked band of fifty men had crept as close to the main gate as possible without being seen. Chretien raised the portcullis, ran down and unbarred the inner doors before the night guards realised what was happening. His fifty shock troops rushed forward, through the main doors, and a pitched battle ensued with the garrison finally aware that they had got a big problem. Although heavily outnumbered Chretien and his small band held the gatehouse area long enough for the main body of troops to reach the fortress and the result was then not in doubt. In accordance with the practices of the time, the garrison were slaughtered to a man and thrown down the well followed by the rubble from the walls that were demolished by the victors. The treasury of the Count of Argenta was removed, with Chretien paying off his men handsomely before loading a wagon, and proceeding on the long journey home."

They had only travelled a short distance from the village when Martin flicked the indicator and turned onto a narrow carriageway that wound through the ubiquitous pine trees for at least two kilometres before emerging into open country. Ahead, on rising ground, could be seen a small fairy tale Chateau complete with turrets. As they drew nearer, Anna could see that originally hidden by a dip in the land was a surrounding wall, and large gates that gave onto a drive leading up to the house. Martin drew to a halt in front of the gates, leapt out and pressed the button on a small speaker unit clamped to the brickwork of the left hand buttress. A brief conversation ensued, and as he walked back to take his seat the gates began to swing slowly open.

Anna could now see that the perimeter wall enclosed a generous amount of land boasting well tended, although not over-manicured, lawns and flower beds. To the right, and set back some ten metres from the drive, was a nicely proportioned detached cottage, beyond which could be seen outbuildings reminiscent of stables although no livestock was apparent. Martin drew to a halt opposite the cottage and, as he again vacated his seat, the door of the cottage opened and an elderly and rather fat man emerged resplendent in beret and blue overalls. He was followed by a slimmer, but not exactly trim, woman of similar age and Anna watched as Martin was now enfolded in the arms of first one then the other, before accepting something that the man pressed into his hand. There was a further five minutes of conversation until he finally walked back to the vehicle and climbed aboard.

"Sorry about that," he said "Marcel and Henrietta were very keen to meet you, but I had to explain that this was merely a working relationship, and that you would make their acquaintance another time."

"I see," said Anna, and couldn't help feeling somewhat hurt that he could not be bothered to make an introduction "Why do they live in the cottage? Is the big house too expensive to run?"

As the Land Rover moved forward Martin shook his head "No, they aren't the owners, they simply look after the house and grounds. Marcel handed me the keys and we will let ourselves in"

"Oh, I see. You've already made all the arrangements for our visit and we are to meet the owner later then?"

They drew to a halt at the foot of the half dozen semi-circular steps that led up to the portico beneath which two stout doors nestled. Martin slipped the key into the lock, pushed the right hand door open and turning to Anna who had followed him said "Actually, I'm the owner."

He disappeared into the spacious entrance hall, strode ahead and, ignoring the elegant staircase that swept upwards to a galleried landing, proceeded through a door at the rear of the hallway and into a large kitchen. "Oh good, looks like 'Etta has done the shopping I asked for. We can survive without having to make a trip back to the village until the evening."

Anna's long legs had carried her hot on Martin's heels, and it was only the astonishment his announcement had caused, that tempered the flash of annoyance she felt rising within her.

"Well thanks for telling me. Is there anything else I should know, I mean if you are really the Baron Sarony incognito please do tell, I can practice curtseying tonight before I go to bed."

Unabashed, he ignored the outburst, liberated a bottle of water from the cavernous inside of a huge refrigerator, poured two glasses and placed them on the table before saying "Sit down and I will put you more fully in the picture, but don't get too sarcastic because, if you recall, it was only this morning that I was made privy to the fact that you were not running back to England after all. Also, you may remember that I offered lunch a couple of weeks back which you turned down on the grounds that we were not 'together'. I had intended telling you the whole story at that time – well in advance of our trip, but you" and here he pointed to emphasise his words – "you declined, and said you didn't want to hear from me until a couple of days before the sailing." He paused then added "So don't act all injured and offended, and I'll now give you the full story."

It was at that point that Anna realised why Martin Price wound her up. It was because he was always bloody well right, and more to the point she always felt like a naughty schoolgirl whenever he pointed it out.

"All right, I'm sorry." Christ, here she was, apologising, when she never did in any other situation. She was usually the one in charge, not some….!

"Ready then?" Realising that she had drifted off and was staring into space, she nodded, and took a sip of water as he started.

"Right, I'll give you a quick background so this will make a bit more sense. My dad died when I was only three years old. He was a professional soldier, and mum then married again having met the already famous archaeologist Armand Furneaux. Although mum was very ill when you met her recently, she had, in her younger years, been a vivacious and attractive woman, and so the second marriage to a distinguished figure like Armand was not too surprising. He was, as you will have realised, her senior by quite a number of years, but they were a good match and their time together was a happy one. It was, however, Armand's death from cancer when I was in my early twenties, which changed my life completely."

He took a drink from his glass and as she said nothing continued the tale. "You are aware of Armand's eminence in our chosen field of course. What you won't know is that not only was he without doubt a very brilliant man, he was also very wealthy. In fact more so than I, and I think mum, actually knew. It was due to him that I originally decided archaeology would also be my forte and, even as a youngster, the Sarony Treasure story intrigued me. What was revealed following Armand's death was the fact that his wealth was considerable, and that he was the owner of Chateau Sarony and its estates. Those estates comprised not just the immediate acreage of the grounds, but also almost the entire village of Sarony itself, and to cap it all he had left the whole caboodle to me – his French Estate that is, mum was of course more than fully taken care of in other areas.

"So your step-father was actually descended from Chretien de Sarony?"

"No, he took the opportunity to acquire the estate from the last of the Sarony heirs back in the 1970's when said heir was teetering on the brink of bankruptcy; shrewd bird was Armand, and it's proved a good long term investment."

"You said his death changed your life," she prompted.

"Yes it did. There was I lumbered with the responsibility of this wretched French chateau and all, and suddenly absolutely loaded. It completely destroyed my perspective and ambition. I didn't need to aspire to follow in Armand's exalted footsteps did I? Why did I need to grub away on little known sites in the middle of nowhere when I had more money than I knew what to do with? Poor little rich boy me, I ran away and joined the army like my real dad would have wanted. I left the estate to be professionally managed for me and only visited during leave periods when I felt like it."

"But then you left the army."

"Yes, when mum was diagnosed with cancer I knew I had to be with her. I wasn't going to have her 'professionally managed' like a French estate, and so, apart from a daytime nurse to cover when I was out working with Mickey, I actually did something worthwhile with my life."

"That was why you flew into a rage in the pub at Grantfield - you had to be back with your mother?"

"Not exactly, I had one last report to pick up based on a new treatment for mum's condition, but it was all too late, the cancer was too advanced. I knew in my heart that would be the case and McEwan just got under my skin at the wrong time.

While mum was ill I did on occasions hire a nurse and take an occasional week's break. Over time I have built up a rapport with quite a few of the local people. When the old boy who used to run the Fleurie said he wanted to retire I decided to take a chance on Monique. She was working in the bar and she needed an incentive to make my investment work for me, so I now own half the Fleurie with Monique. I also employ Marcel and Henrietta to look after the house and grounds and hire whatever labour is needed to keep things in good order."

"Seems an odd way to protect an investment – by giving half away I mean."

"Yes I suppose so, but I meant my whole investment. Monique is young, energetic and running the village auberge there is nothing she does not know about what is going on. I trust her implicitly and so securing her by giving her half of the Fleurie seemed like good business. She couldn't have bought into it as she had no resources of her own, but being there already meant there was continuity and she keeps all of the profits apart from what is needed to maintain the building in good order. I'm a silent partner in the business itself so, if it is ever necessary to sell the Fleurie lock stock and barrel, I should do quite nicely."

Anna judged it wise not to divulge what Monique had already told her about her past, and contented herself by nodding and saying, "So that more or less fills in your background, what about Chretien de Sarony?"

"On one of my visits I found some of Armand's notebooks and discovered that he had started to research the Sarony story, but with mum's illness taking up most of my time I decided to leave any follow-up on the back burner until….., well, until the inevitable occurred. Then when you tried to hire me it reawakened my interest and following mum's death, I realised that if I could get the Uni involved via you and Smiffy, it could help me back into the world of archaeology. I said as much when we were in Smiffy's study if you remember. So now it's my turn to ask a question. What did you mean yesterday when you implied that I was up to something?"

Anna let the question hang in the air for a few seconds before answering, and felt decidedly uncomfortable as she did so. Even so, she did not repeat Rod McEwan's theory and instead presented a watered down explanation.

"To put it bluntly I thought you were trying to push me down the ladder, so far as research into the Sarony Treasure was concerned, because you had found something tangible. I thought you wanted to ensure that if I was playing second fiddle to you then you would get all the credit."

"Blimey, you make me sound like a cross between Machiavelli, and Indiana Jones. Do you really dislike me that much?"

Her mind raced for the right words because it was true that *dislike* was too strong.

"No, of course not. Yesterday was so difficult that I let my imagination run away with me, particularly when you said you could have killed those men if you had wanted to."

"Well that's presenting a different interpretation to the one I recall. It was you who said that I could have killed them, implying that I had somehow gone berserk and lashed out without any thought to the consequences. As if I had done it all because I like hurting people. I said that if I'd wanted to kill them I could have done, meaning that it wouldn't have been an accident."

"A legacy from the army?"

"Yes, controlled violence is part of what good soldiering is about. I did what I thought was required, no more and no less and I can't help it if you don't approve. It's not as if we are anything more than work colleagues, as you have pointed out. Can we now move on to the reason we are here?"

"Fair enough, where do we start?"

Chapter 11 - A Start

He looked at her and grinned.

"Not with our diggers or spades that's for sure. Armand left a few cryptic notes only, but it was enough to convince me that we needed to look here in France, not England. There are three lines in his notes entered as bullet points as the last entries saying 'Why didn't wife and child go to England?' and another that says "Where is son buried?' and finally a third saying "Why sell Sarony House if treasure is in England?'

At this point Martin held up his hand and said "Before you ask to see Armand's notes I should mention two things. Firstly, he wrote in his mother tongue – French, which will not be helpful for you, and secondly, those are the only three lines that directly raise questions. All the rest are notes about the historical evidence that is already in the public domain, mainly concerning the removal of the treasure from Italy and the journey home.

"And that's it?"

"Apart from a few historical source references, yes."

"That is what has convinced you that we should be looking in France rather than England?"

"Yes"

"Well I'm sorry if I'm missing the obvious but I don't see anything to get excited about."

"Fair comment, but you didn't know Armand. These notes were made not very long before he died, and he knew he was dying, but despite everything he added these comments to his research material. So he clearly thought them significant. He wouldn't have done it for fun, and he was meticulous in his work."

"But there is hardly anything at all to go on."

"There is so little because he had only just got going when the illness took hold, and he was making sure that what little he had deduced would be passed on."

"To you?"

"Probably."

"OK, I'll bow to your knowledge of the man. So tell me what we should infer from these few lines and just where we should start. How do we decide what is pertinent and what isn't when we don't even know what we are looking for?"

"Well to my mind the most obvious place to start is the line about why the wife and child didn't go to England because that clearly contradicts the known facts – at least so far as the wife is concerned."

Anna thought for a moment before saying "Yes of course, Chretien and his wife are buried together in the vault beneath St Bertha's aren't they, so why is he saying that she didn't go to France with their son?"

Martin smiled, rose to his feet, and said "Let me show you around the Chateau. We can talk about this as we go. It's not as large as some people would imagine and Marcel and 'Etta only keep the East wing rooms ready for use. All the other upper rooms have their furniture under dust covers, although that will change of course when I take up permanent residence."

They paused in the entrance hall and Anna's gaze was drawn to the staircase and the line of portraits punctuating the wall ascending to the first floor gallery. "Do you think Armand was referring to Chretien's initial journey to England with Henry Tudor and his army? I mean it was a hazardous venture and it wouldn't have been wise for wives and children to accompany the soldiery would it? They weren't common camp followers were they?"

"You're right," agreed Martin "but why would that have been worthy of a note bearing in mind the success at Bosworth, and the fact that she clearly did come to England because they are buried together in Grantfield?"

"But their son apparently didn't, and more to the point Armand wasn't able to trace where he was buried. Of course, we do know that there was no son to claim the Estate following Chretien's death because it passed to a cousin or something. So that would seem to imply that the son either didn't reach majority, or if he did he died before Chretien. Perhaps we should actually concentrate on the son rather than the contradiction concerning the wife."

"Maybe, to tell you the truth Anna I'm not certain there is a good or bad place to start. It's always struck me though, that the statement about the wife not going to England stood out because it was so obviously a contradiction of verified fact, whereas the comments about the son and the sale of the Grantfield property hang together more."

"I'm not sure I follow your reasoning Martin. "How are they linked?"

"Purely by dubious logic I'm afraid, but Armand was very logical. "I think we can take it as read that Chretien outlived his son because his estate in the general sense ended up being claimed by a distant relative. That was possible because his wife had pre-deceased him and there was no son able to inherit. The weakness of this, as Armand's notes seem to point out, is that he had not been able to track down where the son was buried so was unable to verify the boy's death beyond doubt. Now I can tell you that during the centuries from Chretien's death until Armand purchased what remained of the French estate, the Sarony family were not good with money. What was once a wealthy landowning family, holding very large and extensive property, gradually sold off chunks of its portfolio over the years until what is left is now owned by me – a person with no connection to the old family."

"I don't see why that is relevant" commented Anna.

"As I said earlier, it's dubious logic, but if we assume that the cousin who was fortunate enough to inherit Chretien's possessions was himself of this spendthrift mentality, then that would fit very nicely with the fact that the first thing he seems to have done once he inherited, is flog the English properties, quite possibly to give himself some ready money. More to the point however, is that if we, at a distance of over five hundred years, are aware of the story regarding a great treasure, how much more aware would this cousin have been? So logically there is no way on God's earth that he would have flogged the English possessions if he thought there was the faintest chance of the treasure being in England."

"Ah yes, and now I see why you said you thought looking for it in Grantfield was a waste of time," mused Anna. "By the way, which of these is Chretien?" She waved vaguely at the portraits lining the staircase.

"Oh he's part of the family group at the top. Look I'll show you."

She followed him and he paused at the top of the stairs by a large portrait of a knight in doublet and hose, smiling out at them with his left hand on the shoulder of his seated wife who in turn held on her lap an infant of about three years of age. Affixed to the imposing ornate frame were the words 'Chretien Comte de Sarony, Mathilde Eugenie de Sarony, Francois Alexandre de Sarony'.

"Is this a fifteenth century painting?" she asked.

"Yes, I think so. It's by an anonymous artist and not particularly good so not valuable - like all of the others here. Anything of real value was sold by the previous owners, and I understand from Marcel that when Armand bought the place, he found all of these old paintings in one of the attics gathering dust. He had them cleaned up and lined the staircase with them just for decoration."

They moved on and he showed Anna the four bedrooms, three bathrooms and dayroom adjoining the master bedroom that formed the east wing. A floor to ceiling window cast daylight into the long corridor and at the very end, to the right of the window, was a narrow door. When opened, this disclosed an equally narrow spiral staircase leading up to a small turret room that Martin referred to as an attic. The house itself was laid out in the form of a geometric U shape with the South facing centre section providing the façade housing the main front doors through which they had first entered, and two reception rooms. There was no corresponding parallel rear section, and so what could have been an enclosed quadrangle was instead open to views across the countryside beyond, with an extensive rear terrace and ornamental flower beds occupying the centre area between the wings and the southern cross-section. This layout became evident to Anna as she examined the view to be had from each of the slit windows of the circular 'attic'.

She suddenly recalled a comment he had made earlier and said "You intend to come and live here then?"

"Yes, it would seem foolish not to, don't you think? I mean to say, I feel I have a stronger connection with this area than Grantfield. During my army days I moved around quite a bit and didn't really put roots down anywhere. Mum's illness and my decision to look after her restricted my social life, but having got married and then divorced whilst I was in the army I can't say I was desperate for a vibrant personal life. As a result I've got quite a few more friends here than in England."

"Like Monique?"

He looked at her sharply, and she wondered if she had said the wrong thing, but his face relaxed into a smile as he said. "Yes she is my closest friend. Now what about giving me a bit of information about Anna Freemont? We appear to have lasted the morning without tearing each others throats out, but I know nothing about you, do I?"

She hesitated before answering "There's not a great deal to tell. Daddy is headmaster at a small private school and mummy works as curator of the Grantfield and District Museum. I was educated at Millies – that's St Millicent's to you, went to Reading and got a second in archaeology. Mummy knew of a vacancy coming up at Grantfield Uni and Professor Smithson-Hunt's predecessor took me on. I've never been married, had one or two longish term boyfriends, and now at the age of twenty six I'm hoping to move forward in my profession. No current boyfriend, although Rod McEwan would like to change that, except I don't actually like him that much. I was head girl at school, and I was hoping that having been taken on as senior assistant in the department I would eventually be entrusted with something that would establish my name. I think the Professor felt that heading up the Sarony House research dig would put me on that road."

As she was speaking they had descended from the attic, made their way through the corridor and back down the stairs to the entrance hall.

"Fancy a glass of wine with lunch?" asked Martin "'Etta has put all sorts of goodies in the fridge including some local white stuff that should be nicely chilled. Then I thought we could have a dig in the library to see if we could locate the sources used by Armand."

"Wine and lunch would be nice thanks, but library?"

"Coming up. Yes, library here in the chateau, second door on the right when you come into the hall. Quite a lot of old stuff there that I haven't ever had time to go through, and then Armand added his books, so we've probably got as good a collection of reference books concerning archaeology in general, and Chateau Sarony in particular, as anywhere. But there is always our old friend the internet to fall back on if needs be. I had a decent PC and broadband and whatnot installed not long ago, and there are a couple of laptops in addition to the one you've got in your rucksack."

"They had just sat down when a loud knocking on the front door brought Martin to his feet and hurrying from the kitchen. Anna briefly heard a man's voice drift from the front door before footsteps signified his return.

"Sorry about that" he said as he poured them both a generous glass of wine to accompany the cold meat salad. "Just Marcel with my keys."

"Didn't you collect them when we arrived?"

"House keys yes, car keys no. I keep a modern four wheel drive here and just use the old Land Rover for transporting Mickey on his trailer, and buzzing around Grantfield."

"More rattling than buzzing" quipped Anna and Martin stopped with his glass half raised to his lips and said "You know, that's the first light hearted thing I've heard you say since I met you in Grantfield."

She felt her face flush red and answered "Yes, well until today we don't ever seem to have really hit it off do we. But tell me, why have you opted to stay at the auberge and not here?"

"Well I always like to have a night with Monique, we sometimes don't get to sleep until three or four o'clock and….." he stopped at the look on her face and burst out laughing. "I didn't mean *that* Anna, although there have been past occasions when we have drunk a little too much, and well, things do occasionally just take on a momentum all their own don't they."

"A bit like Nikki-with-two-kays?" The words were out before she could stop them and she saw the smile fade from his face.

He leaned forward and said, "First of all, Monique – she is my friend and she keeps me up to date with village matters as I told you. The fact that she is very attractive and has a body to die for is just a lucky coincidence of nature."

"As for Nikki – her surname is Prendergast by the way – she is very aware that you academic lot take the piss behind her back, but that hasn't stopped one or two of your male colleagues trying to get into her knickers it seems. I had a most enjoyable lunch with Nikki who thinks that you, Anna, are the most beautiful thing on two legs. She told me I should try and take advantage of the fact that you were single before somebody else did."

Once again she heard herself say "Sorry" and once again the smile returned as he said "Forget it, I'm really not a devious character you know, but I admit I thought that if I owned up to the fact I was the owner of Chateau Sarony, and suggested we stay here, you might easily have got the wrong idea. That was the main reason for booking the auberge, I can catch up with Monique's news anytime as we are here for a few weeks. What you see is more or less what you get, so come on, be a good colleague and help me launch an assault on Armand's library."

They walked through to the library, which although not vast, certainly contained many hundreds of books. The room was dominated by several large windows beneath which ran a window-seats topped by a comfortable looking hassock. The walls to the right and left were lined with floor to ceiling shelves that accommodated an impressive array of volumes of varying sizes and bindings. A mahogany desk and captain's chair faced the window, and a substantial chandelier looked more than able to illuminate even the furthest recesses. A state of the art pc with a massive monitor occupied a smaller work station set to one side of the desk, and the furnishings were completed by two four-seat settees and two easy chairs.

"I'm afraid that most of the books are........."

"In French" she completed. "So why don't we see what we can find in Armand's notes, and I'll see if I can find English versions on the internet and where possible download them. You concentrate on anywhere there is no English version, because I am sure your comprehension of the French written word is as sickeningly fluent as your verbal ability."

"That's two" he said.

"Too well organised?"

"No - two jokes since we've met" he replied as he turned to activate the PC, and consequently missed the very unladylike gesture that she made behind his back.

The rest of that afternoon was spent following up the book titles noted in the Furneaux notebook which resulted in Anna being able to download three titles to her tablet, while Martin plucked several hardback volumes from the library shelves and stacked them neatly beside the settee. Their day finished with the short ride back to Auberge Fleurie in Martin's top of the range BMW X3 which Anna commented, perhaps unwisely, didn't give her a flat bum like the old Land Rover. Martin's riposte to the effect that after careful study her bum had never looked flat to him was delivered in such a deadpan manner that she could not decide whether he was joking, or passing a serious anatomical verdict.

There was a large family dinner party at the auberge and Monique was kept busy supervising so was unable to join them. They spent a subdued dinner as the day's activities, combined with the additional strain as they each carefully avoided areas of potential conflict, had tired them out. All the remaining guest rooms were taken and the late night banging of doors and alcohol induced foolish behaviour cut their sleep and propelled them down to breakfast the following morning in a state of bleary eyed grumpiness.

"I hope we don't have any more nights like that" moaned Anna.

"Can't be guaranteed now the season's started I'm afraid," he replied, then added "We could sleep at the chateau from tonight onwards. It's far more comfortable and you could have the bedroom nearest the gallery, which means you won't hear me snoring in the master bedroom. Also you will have your own bathroom at no extra charge."

She smiled and asked "Won't Monique be offended?"

"Good heavens no, when I first booked she was convinced that I was being discrete to spare your feelings and that we would be surreptitiously creeping around the upstairs corridor in the avid pursuit of rampant sex. It took me ages to convince her that the chances of that happening were about as likely as it suddenly raining lemonade. What's up? You've gone a bit red."

"Nothing's up, and I agree that it would be silly not to stay at the chateau. I've never stayed in a chateau so it will be a bit of a treat and, as there is no danger of me being ravished by the evil master of the house, I will relish a comfortable night's sleep for the first time since arriving in France."

A puzzled expression appeared on his face "But you said you slept like a log the night before last."

"No Martin, you must have misheard me. Now look, I've been giving our project a good deal of thought and wonder if it would be more worthwhile if we were to start our research by trying to track the journey that Chretien and his treasure took from Italy back to Sarony?"

The following day breakfast was eaten on the terrace at the rear of the chateau as Anna stretched her legs and slouched in her chair. The morning sun washed the dullness from her body as she contentedly licked the remnants of a buttered croissant from her fingers. She watched Martin covertly watching her from behind his familiar slit eyed pose of insouciance that she now knew camouflaged an intent focus on his immediate surroundings. Finally his voice drifted across the rustles, clicks, and buzzes of the garden's permanent inhabitants:

"Well are you going to tell me more about your research suggestion last night or do we opt for starting with the youngster?"

She regarded him silently for a long half minute before launching onto the warm morning air the thoughts which had coalesced overnight into a firm opinion. Martin had waited without further comment for almost 24 hours as she failed to amplify on her suggestion regarding the starting point for their field work. For the first time in many months her nerves felt less ragged, and with some surprise she realised how much she liked the fact that he never did try to chase an answer but, instead, simply assumed that if he waited long enough then a response would be forthcoming. This was what had originally made her feel uneasy in his presence, not the grey eyes, nor the undefined something behind them, but the tension he seemed able to create by waiting and saying nothing.

She sat herself upright and looked steadily at him before saying "I think it will be a mistake to try and follow a path that we think can be initiated from Armand's notes. We have no way of knowing if his own thought process proceeded in any particular direction, so it is simply a lottery. We would just be taking pot shots at what he believed to be salient facts without having a clue to how they became so.

Most of the literature I have read recently concentrates on what Chretien could possibly have done with his loot *after* his return home. Opinion seems divided but I think I will join with you in the view that it did not end up in England.

Now it's not as if we have got several possible sites to start investigating is it? All we have got amounts to nothing more than a strong rumour. Even the actual existence of the treasure is disputed in some quarters, and so my feelings are that we need to boil this thing down to a firmer set of data. I think that the Count of Argenta did lose a fortune at Frosinone due to Chretien. We know that the action at Frosinone is an historical event. We know that Chretien hauled a cartload of something almost 400 miles from Italy to Sarony as evidenced by a number of, admittedly sketchy, historical accounts.

So instead of starting off on a random basis with one of the many things we DONT know, I think we should start with something we *do* know. As luck would have it, here we are actually based in Chateau Sarony, at the heart of the entire story, so there is the obvious temptation for us to focus on this area but, perversely, this is the area of Chretien's adventure that we know least about. So I think we should start from the opposite direction, concentrate on the verified fact of the journey itself which took several months, and see if anything new turns up. If we can follow his trail from Italy to Sarony we may somehow gain further clues or insights into how he managed to conceal the treasure so effectively.

Even in the fifteenth century, Europe was more populous than most areas, and yet he was apparently able to bring this hoard hundreds of miles to Sarony, secrete it without leaving any clues, and five hundred years later, despite the population in the area greatly increasing, no hint of it's location has ever surfaced."

She felt pleased that she had managed to steer her mind back into professional thinking mode and waited for his reaction.

He nodded and said "So we start in Italy and wend our way back across France in the footsteps of our hero for a distance of about 400 miles, and see if we can somehow build up a picture?"

"What I suggest is, that we try and draft a probable route that Chretien could have taken based on the geographical references we can find in Armand's notes and any of the sources he mentions. Then we actually visit the site of the stronghold at Frosinone and look over whatever remains, plus, check out any local historical archives. From there we try and travel by whatever route we think is closest to Chretien's passage to the next place we have pencilled in as a likely stopping-off point, and repeat the process until we get back here. If we turn up any new information on our travels that changes our projected route back to Sarony, we can adapt our plans. It may prove to be a dead end, but at least we will have tried an alternative approach."

"OK Anna, that's a nice idea. I like the logic and it is certainly something different to my own initial reasoning. If we take a couple of days to work out a route map for ourselves and, say, two to drive to Frosinone. Hmm, then it could take as much as seven days to amble back, so we will have used up eleven days at least on the whole trip. Are you sure you want to try it?"

"On one condition only" she answered.

"And that is?"

"That we travel in the Beamer and not the Land Rover."

Chapter 12 - Pont de Tresor

The next two days saw them spend almost their entire time in the library, with Martin giving Anna excerpts from the Furneaux notes so that she could follow leads via her laptop. He then concentrated on the French language books, and other literature referenced by his late step-father, whilst accessing the PC to provide assistance when necessary. They were kept regularly supplied with food and drink by Marcel whom, in going about his work in the grounds, would occasionally linger beneath the windows of the first floor bedrooms in the hope of catching those sounds which indicate a man and woman enjoying more than a purely working relationship. When 'Marti' had arrived with the tall blonde, both Marcel and Henrietta had assumed a level of intimacy that was not yet evident, despite Marcel's careful eavesdropping, and a close examination of the bed linen by Henrietta.

In many ways the attitude of the Sarony village residents had remained unchanged for centuries. The village was still for the most part owned by the owner of the chateau, and so too were a number of the outlying farms. When the last of the Sarony heirs sold his interest to the famous professor, they had hoped the chateau would remain occupied, but the professor spent more time away from the chateau than actually in occupation, and it was managed over the years on his behalf by a number of estate managers. When the estate was inherited by the old professor's step-son hopes were again raised, but visits from the young owner had been infrequent until the last couple of years. The fact was that for as long as records had been kept, the village and its farms had looked to the chateau for leadership and guidance. Even in these modern times this traditional, almost visceral need for the owner of the chateau to act as a father figure was still very much a part of every Sarony resident's psyche. That the present owner was English, rather than French, was unfortunate, and the fact that he was unmarried, doubly so.

This latter state could however change, and although not a Frenchman the young owner had eventually begun to spend more frequent periods in Sarony and develop friendships and connections within the local community. The fact that he spoke fluent French did him no harm and when word inevitably spread that he was prevented from taking up permanent residence due to having to care for his dying mother his stock soared. This was something the traditionally minded Sarony residents could appreciate, in fact it was exactly the behaviour they would expect from the owner of the château. When it became known that the mother had died, hopes had again risen and had now reached an almost feverish state of optimism - thanks to the arrival of the statuesque blonde.

It was against this background of community expectation that Marcel felt no sense of disloyalty as he was deployed, under the watchful gaze of 'Etta, as the first line of investigation into the status of the blonde.

The hard work of the two persons at the heart of this local interest resulted in a miserly four stops being identified as verified locations at which Chretien had camped on his journey from Frosinone. When they finally set off on the journey to Italy and turned onto the road for Dijon Martin commented "This may turn out to be a quicker trip than we expected, but at least in a few minutes time you will be able to see our famous local landmark."

"That's not the chateau then?"

"Nope, it's the Pont de Tresor"

"Well, even my embarrassingly limited knowledge of French can manage Treasure Bridge. It is obviously connected in some way with Chretien isn't it, but how come it has that name?"

At this point she saw that a few hundred yards ahead, their road continued across a stone bridge which from its appearance was centuries old. Martin halted the car at a parking space just before the bridge and they made their way forward onto one of the narrow paved footways that were barely wider than a human body and ran either side of the single lane road. They gingerly walked in single file to the first of the stone balconies that bulged from the parapet and afforded space for two persons to stand to admire the surroundings. The bridge itself was no more than two hundred feet in length and there were three of the stone vantage points on each side. Looking west, they saw the pine clad slopes gradually falling away until they levelled out and the trees gave way to gently undulating farmland. To the East, the trees also petered out, but this was due to the terrain changing to increasingly steep rocky hillsides divided by the ravine that wound into the distant hills. Beneath them ran the river Tarbe and even in their elevated position the hissing and crashing of it's passage could be heard.

"That's a long drop," said Anna as she gazed down at the river some three hundred feet below.

He nodded "Yes, and to answer your earlier question, this bridge does owe its name to the treasure that we are hoping to track down. But it's not the original bridge from Chretien's day, that was a wooden structure, and this bridge, ancient as it is, merely inherited the name."

Leaning across the parapet Anna peered along the outer length of the bridge and noted the stone gutters that with gargoyle style embellishments protruded from the centre of each balcony just below the level of their feet. Looking back down inside the balcony she noted the holes that allowed excess rain water to drain down into the protruding gutters.

Martin interrupted her thoughts by saying "Local legend has it that Chretien's treasure consisted of holy artefacts, gold chalices etc and holy relics and that as he was crossing the bridge his conscience got the better of him and he chucked all of his sacrilegious loot over the side and it disappeared into the river."

"You don't think that's possible?"

"Well I don't believe that there were any religious items, I think that is just some fanciful story that adds a little mystique to what was only ever a local rumour."

"So there's no chance that the treasure went over the side?"

"It's possible alright, but unlikely. He was a tough character and I don't see him lugging it all that way and then dumping it within sight of home. In any case, the only likely reason for him suddenly going all soppy and doing that would be if there really was that religious angle. Whatever constituted the Argenta treasury I'm pretty sure it wasn't a load of gold chalices. Gold and silver coinage would be my best guess.

"Just a romantic story then, in your opinion?"

"Yes, I don't think it stands up to any objective test. Besides, a ton of gold whether it be sacred bits and pieces or sacks of coin is unlikely to disappear without trace in those circumstances is it? We may be a long way above the level of a rapidly moving river but, even in those far off days, word would have soon got round and a great deal of jettisoned valuables soon recovered. Gold and silver are powerful motivators. No, I'm sure we can chalk that one off our list of probable solutions."

As they walked back to the car she said "The little girl in me would like it to be true but I must reluctantly agree that you are right Martin. It's a good story to start our journey with though."

As they moved off and Martin eased the vehicle across the bridge, she slipped on her sunglasses, tilted her seat back slightly, and reflected on recent events. How different it was to be snuggled comfortably in the X3 feeling relaxed when compared to the tense discomfort of the Land Rover journey a few days ago. Her thoughts were interrupted by Martin saying "We are just about to go through Colmierre and, although it isn't mentioned in either Armand's notes or other sources as an overnight stop, there is no doubt that Chretien passed through here and did stop, even if only for an hour or two. Depending on the time of day he may even have stayed overnight."

"So close?" She asked in surprise.

"He was driving an ox-cart so, typically, with a pair as the engine room, he could have covered 10 miles per day, but with a ton of gold on board 4 or 5 miles is more likely."

They exited Colmierre and he swung the X3 onto the road that was signposted for the auto route.

"So he would have taken say 100 days to complete the journey."

"Longer I think," he responded. "He may well have rested on Sundays like a good Christian, and that would have benefited the oxen. Add in, say, another 10 days for accidents, illness and such like, and you have got a journey of more like 125 days. He would have been anxious to press on, but say 4 months in all, which I think more or less fits the time from the short siege at Frosinone to his recorded instructions to the innkeeper north of Colmierre for one of those wayside shrines to be constructed in thanksgiving for a safe journey."

"Why Colmierre and not Sarony?"

"Nothing much at Sarony in those days. Not even a church, whereas Colmierre was already an established village. I expect he gave thanks in the chapel at the chateau though."

"I didn't know there was a chapel at the chateau Martin."

"There isn't any longer. Napoleon's lads destroyed it."

Chapter 13 - Italy

Frosinone was a disappointment, consisting of only a small village and very little information regarding the stronghold that once held the Argenta Treasury. It was only after asking an elderly shopkeeper that they were able to locate the original site some two miles from the village itself. Even then, they were forced to park the vehicle and hike across two fields of lavender before trudging to the top of the hill that hundreds of years before had echoed to the sound of battle and the cries of the wounded and dying.

"Less than inspiring" was Martin's comment.

They surveyed the rutted hilltop from which chunks of masonry breaking the surface could be spotted at certain points among the tall windswept grass tufts. A closer inspection combined with much tramping around in the knee high grass enabled them to gain some idea of where the ancient walls had once both protected and defied armed and armoured soldiery.

"It looks completely neglected," commented Anna as she surveyed the desolate scene. Did they never attempt to rebuild it?"

"Doesn't look like it does it? I reckon that this is almost untouched since the day Chretien pulled out. No doubt most of the movable masonry was put to other uses. It would be interesting to have a tour of the local farmhouses and barns to see how much of the old stronghold can be located."

"I'm surprised at how little the locals have made of the story, there's no sign of any tourist literature nor any mention of the existence of the site itself for the benefit of would-be visitors. It's clearly not rated at all as having any genuine historical or archaeological significance" answered Anna.

Martin shaded his eyes as he gazed in the direction of France and then turned to his companion saying, "That's because it's a French story and the Italians were never really aware of the so called treasure. For them this is just the location of a minor event that is completely dwarfed by their own towering history. The story of the French knight and his supposed treasure originated in France and was for several hundred years no more than a local rumour in the Sarony area."

Looking out from the hilltop and across the surrounding countryside Anna inhaled deeply and remarked "It's a nice spot with a good view, but short of undertaking a full scale dig I don't think we are going to learn much from this site. Mind you, it's quite romantic, thinking that Chretien may once have gazed out at exactly the same view don't you think? Why are you looking at me like that Martin?"

"No reason, other than I hadn't really got you pegged as the romantic type, but I totally agree with you about the site. Let's get over to Campomorto tomorrow and see if there is anything of interest there shall we? Then we can move on to Vigevano, it's only about 25 miles further on and so it's a nice easy start to our route." He turned and began to descend and so missed the muttered comment from Anna as she stared at his retreating back.

"I'm as bloody romantic as the next woman. Maybe I just need someone who brings it to the surface," and she stomped grumpily down the hillside in his wake.

She was still simmering as they drove to Campomorto, during which time he glanced at her once or twice and wondered what he had now managed to say or do that had driven his prickly companion into another introspective silence. Recalling all too clearly the combustible nature of her moods he elected to remain in watchful anticipation rather than fuel any latent flames. They drove some distance in this state of motorised tension but her mood appeared to slowly thaw as she sat behind her sunglasses and surveyed the rolling Italian countryside. He was relieved to see that by the time they reached Campomorto it was evident from her body language that the moodiness had subsided. Entering the outskirts of the town they easily found a parking spot and decided to walk through to the centre. In such a small place it only took a few minutes and it was when they reached the central Piazza Ferrara that Anna spotted a tourist information centre. Having been elected expedition linguist Martin volunteered to see what he could find, as Anna smirked in triumph at having secured the onerous duty of selecting which of the three bars surrounding the square should provide their lunch.

He entered the gloomy interior of the tourist information centre, which also doubled as the local newsagent, and looked around. Despite his calm and almost languid appearance he was feeling irritated by the unpredictable character of his travelling companion. Admittedly, she was a striking looking woman and, contrary to his character assessment when he first saw her in Grantfield, she made no attempt to trade on her looks. There were no upturned doe eyes gazing from beneath batted eyelids, in fact no pretence of coyness at all. To her credit she acted as if completely unaware of her good looks but it was a great pity that she frequently also displayed a stiff and rather over sensitive reaction to people in general, and at times outright hostility towards a certain Martin Price in particular. The thoughts drifted along at the back of his mind during the course of the next ten minutes as he managed by way of some rusty Italian, and some fatally fractured English enthusiastically offered by the assistant behind a desk, to obtain three slightly dated brochures detailing the delights of Campomorto. He finally emerged blinking into the sunlight clutching his trophies, and stood for a moment scanning the square for a clue to Anna's choice of eating house.

She was not difficult to spot. On the right hand side of the square was a bar painted in green and red, and there at a table on the pavement sat Anna in the presence of three young men whom, judging by their looks were in their early twenties. He mooched across to the bar and waved the brochures in his hand as he caught Anna's eye. Her table was fully occupied so he sat at the adjoining one, and when she showed no indication that she would join him he said

"Are you having lunch with me or staying with your new friends?"

"Of course not, they just plonked themselves down and when I tried to indicate that I was waiting for someone they didn't understand. I've had to sit here and suffer being chatted up in a foreign language, and to be honest there have been a couple of attempts at physical contact such as hand touching that are beginning to irritate."

"You could always have come over to the shop couldn't you?"

She glared at him "Why should I? I chose this spot before these fellows turned up, and it's not as if I'm entitled to run to you for protection like some helpless wife or girlfriend."

"That's true, so as an independent woman not looking for protection why don't you now change tables? We don't need to get involved with your admirers and we need to look through these brochures."

"There's no need for sarcasm," she retorted but did as he suggested to the accompaniment of theatrical groans from her erstwhile table companions. They had only just spread the brochures out onto the table when within seconds Anna was struck on the head by a peanut, soon to be followed by another which bounced on the table in front of Martin. Both missiles had been launched against a background of whistles and kissing sounds from the young men.

Martin straightened up in his chair and Anna saw the affability disappear from his eyes as her stomach clenched. Turning to stare at the most heavily built of the three young men he said something in slow deliberate Italian, and accompanied his comments by the set look that she had come to dread seeing appear on his face. The man flushed red and half rose from his seat only to sit back down again as Martin slowly shook his head and spoke a little more in the Latin tongue. A tense silence descended as the two others shifted uncomfortably in their seats and with a sudden movement that made her jump all three got to their feet, said something to her in Italian, and walked off.

Martin turned back to her and said "Now where were we, what's the matter? You've gone white as a sheet, where's the waiter – ah, about time."

The welcome interruption gave her a chance to gather her wits and discreetly ease her sweaty palms along her thighs to dry them. Drinks soon arrived in response to Martin's urgent words that had sent the waiter scurrying back into the café, and as he fussed around and insisted she drank some chilled water her nerves steadied and she said.

"I'm fine thanks Martin, really I am. Those guys were just getting on my nerves that's all. What did you say to them?"

He looked questioningly at her before suddenly smiling and saying,

"My Italian leaves a lot to be desired especially as I seldom use it, but I managed to explain that flicking peanuts at us was a contravention of the Health and Safety rules"

"Health and Safety?"

"Theirs"

"You mean you threatened to beat them up?"

"Not at all, I don't pick fights with children. I simply told them that it would be a kind gesture if they were to move on."

She flashed a suspicious look at him and said "And what did they say to me as they were leaving?"

"My Italian's a bit rusty as I said, but I think that they quite liked the look of you so I suppose it was complimentary."

He grinned and flipped a brochure across the table to her, saying "Look, they've got a small museum that is only open two days per week and one of them is today. Let's order and after eating take a look shall we?"

The museum was a single story prefabricated building tucked away down a nondescript side street and consisted mainly of a large room holding twenty old fashioned glass display cases. In a corner at the rear they could see a glazed cubicle occupied by a solitary figure in the pale blue uniform of a local government official, busily tapping away at a PC. He seemed unaware of their presence as with deeply furrowed brow he stabbed occasionally at his keyboard with the forefinger of either hand. It was a curious sight and reminded Anna of a bird pecking at ground food.

They made their way slowly among the cases but disappointingly only one proved to hold items connected to Chretien de Sarony. This contained a large and rusted key, a broken and discoloured gauntlet with three of the finger plates missing, and photographs of half a dozen 15th century documents that according to the display description were bills of sale. When Martin read the text out to Anna he explained that they referred to purchases by Chretien of a string of supplies and an ox. He hauled out his mobile phone and managed to photograph the items before the official called out something in Italian and pointed to a spot above the entry door, which Martin translated as saying that photographs were not allowed. They smiled, shrugged and Anna waved cheerily at the man as they retreated into the bright sunlight of the street. Their stroll back to the car was uneventful apart from another brief encounter with Anna's admirers from the café, who were standing outside an ice-cream parlour. As they walked past, one of the men made a loud comment that brought chuckles from his companions.

"Was that directed to me?" she asked.

"Hmm, sort of, more about you than to you."

"Well?"

"You've got a great bum."

"I beg your pardon!"

"That's what he said, you did ask."

As they strapped themselves into the X3, it was the faintest trace of a smirk on Martin's face that made Anna wonder whether truly accurate translation by him was something she could rely upon in every instance. The engine purred into life and she waited for the aircon to kick in as they pulled out of Campomorto.

Chapter 14 - Poligny

Three days later they arrived in Poligny. This meant that the final leg of their journey back to Sarony could be accomplished within a day, even allowing for a stop at Colmierre. It could not be said that the few hundred miles they had travelled since leaving Campomorto was anything more than geographically educational. They had tried to guess at the probable route taken by Chretien and his small party, but apart from enjoying the countryside and sampling the food, drink and accommodation offered by village inns there was very little to show for their efforts. There really were no additional clues to be found that cast any further light on the journey of the Comte de Sarony back in the late fifteenth century.

The fact that Armand Furneaux had referred to contemporary comments made by two men-at-arms who had accompanied Chretien, was only helpful to the extent that it confirmed the four stopping-off places between Frosinone and Sarony that were actually known. The comments were casual references only, taken from letters written during the following ten years. One by Reynard Longeville mentioned that,

'Chretien bought a pair of oxen and cart from a farmer at Frosinone. The journey taken on our way back from Frosinone was slow with the oxen plodding steadily along under their heavy load. The small and badly maintained bridges at Tessy, Poligny and Tavaux proved particularly troublesome and did not help our good *humour over the weeks we spent on our road home. Tavaux for me was the place where I bade farewell to Chretien and, with my reward safely in the saddle bags aboard the donkey Melissa, I commenced the final portion of my journey.'*

"Useful bloke that Reynard" said Martin as he lounged back in his chair at the small hotel in Poligny. "He not only mentioned three of the places they stopped at, but seems to confirm that they had got something valuable on board. The reference to saddle bags is what makes me think it was more likely to be coin rather than anything else."

"What about the other chap who was with them?" asked Anna as she relaxed in the afternoon sun.

"That would be Gilbert Proudhomme, who left them at Tessy. He is far less verbose and simply says in a letter to his brother shortly after his return *'the oxen were still not fully at ease and our road from Vigevano was more difficult as a result.'* Then in another letter he mentions in passing *'I never did see Chretien again after I left his company at Tessy,'* and that's it from him."

"I was hoping we would pick up some trace of these two companions and perhaps find out a little more than Armand had managed," said Anna. "So let's hope our last stop at Tavaux yields some dividends, because having tramped around Poligny this morning I'm getting a bit despondent. Chretien didn't exactly cut a swathe of fame on his journey back through France did he? If he was looking for a cloak of anonymity then he certainly appears to have achieved his aim.

"Yes, so far we haven't added much to our store of knowledge apart from getting some appreciation of the difficulties of the journey. I suppose the frustration of having to accompany an ox cart trudging along at a snails pace was offset by the knowledge that they had something of great value on board. Those knights of old were the most formidable fighting units then in existence, and must have presented a superb deterrent to any would-be bandits." He scratched at his chin and added "I guess they succeeded and, if as a result nothing noteworthy occurred, then there is unlikely to be anything for us to uncover over five centuries later."

"It was always a long shot hoping to pick up a five hundred year old trail simply by trying to re-trace it though. I don't know what made me suggest it." she said disconsolately.

"We took a chance, we both knew it was a long shot. Even so Anna, I liked the oblique line of thought that we ought to try from an alternative direction. We'll see if we get anywhere at Tavaux tomorrow and also Colmierre. Let's have a good meal in the hotel restaurant this evening to celebrate our anniversary."

"What are you talking about Martin?"

"I'm referring to the fact that today is the fifth whole day that we've managed to get through without having an argument."

She grimaced and replied "We came close that day back in Campomorto though."

"Only because you thought I was going to start a fight with the local half-wits."

"And instead you turned out to be a born again pacifist, although I'm not sure you actually gave me an accurate translation of what you said to them. Would you honestly have taken on three of them if they had turned nasty?"

The dreaded 'look' briefly returned as he said "They didn't have the guts to start anything, and besides, they wouldn't have stood their ground. There was never any danger of a real fight."

"That's what scares me about you Martin, you are so confident that you never seem to back off. You just assume that you will prevail regardless of the opposition."

"I don't see what is so frightening about that, it's not as if I go looking for trouble. I mean, take Campomorto for example. Supposing you and I had been a married couple, or any sort of couple come to that? Those plonkers didn't know what our status was, but it didn't stop them from pushing their luck on the basis that there were three of them and they could be as boorish as they liked. So no, I'm not going to knuckle under to that sort of behaviour because, contrary to biblical opinion, the meek don't inherit the Earth, they just get kicked in the bollocks. But I will concede one thing, as we seem to be on the fringe of an argument."

"And what's that?" Anna replied a little more sharply than she intended.

"The Italians do know a great bum when they see one."

For a moment he wondered if perhaps he had gone too far as she stared at him and he saw her mouth tighten. It was a very long few seconds of silence and then she burst out laughing.

"You cheeky bastard, just for that I'm going to stick you for a bloody expensive bottle of wine at dinner."

Chapter 15 - A Visitor

It is only possible on very rare occasions to identify the precise moment when a relationship changes. When asked in later years about his feelings for Anna, Martin always said it was when she called him a 'cheeky bastard' that he realised the hostility, which had so markedly defined her approach to him from the outset, had been put to one side.

Dinner was a success. The hotel restaurant was no more than pleasant, but the food was excellent. As a bonus, the wine was as good as you expect it be when you are buying it in France from somewhere that is not merely a tourist outlet. The conversation, although heavily biased towards archaeology, also covered their childhood years, growing up, and all the usual details that two people tend to exchange when they begin to lay foundations on which something of more than superficial substance may be built. Aided by the socially liberating affects of good French wine the conversation flowed back and forth on a suddenly unfettered tide of mutual openness. The only area that was what Anna began to define as 'off limits', was any fine detail of Martin's army career, although he was quite candid about his marriage and subsequent divorce, both of which had occurred during his time in uniform. Although he also appeared to be just as forthcoming about having spent almost ten years 'with the colours', as he jokingly referred to his military service, she soon realised that the friends he had in those days were only referred to by their first names. Specific places, regiments, ranks and service specialities were never mentioned. Gentle probing was just as gently deflected, and when her straight question 'what did you do in the army?' was smilingly answered by a simple 'I served in an infantry regiment', she knew that he was very politely telling her to back off. In the end she decided to respect his unspoken need for privacy and let the conversation move to pastures new. She would have loved to learn more, or would she? Perhaps the time was not right and after all, they were no more than colleagues attempting to extract some pleasure from a hitherto fraught working relationship.

The hotel grounds were large and, with dinner satisfyingly completed, it was agreed that on such a beautiful evening a stroll through the extensive, well tended gardens would be welcome, to be followed by coffee on the terrace overlooking the surrounding countryside.

The gravelled pathway beneath their feet scrunched pleasantly, the comfortably cool evening air carried her happy laughter across a manicured lawn as he finished an amusing story from his university days. A middle aged couple observed them from one of the several benches available for the use of hotel visitors, and commented approvingly on the picture presented by the nice looking man and his strikingly attractive companion.

Walking, talking, laughing and generally relaxing puts people at ease with one another and they were only part of the way along the outward leg of their planned walk when, without thinking, Anna slipped her hand inside her companion's upper arm and felt her pulse rate increase as her fingers clasped the firm muscle. If he was surprised he gave no indication, but kept his hand thrust into the pocket of his trousers which meant that she automatically moved closer and their shoulders rubbed as they walked. The conversation continued, but now in a more desultory fashion as thoughts became less synchronised with speech, while they each sought to exert some control over the evening's developments.

"This is a marvellous evening," he said as they approached the terrace from the rose garden by the lower lake.

"Wonderful temperature even now," she agreed.

"I wasn't just referring to the surroundings, I haven't dared to move my right arm for the last half hour in case you took your hand away."

"You don't mind me grabbing hold of you like some needy old spinster then?"

He chuckled, withdrew his hand from his pocket and slipped it lightly around her waist as they ascended the steps to the rear terrace. Neither of them noticed the solitary figure sitting at one of the wrought iron tables.

How their evening may then have unfolded they would never know because they had only taken a few paces towards a table at the back of the terrace when a familiar voice broke into the softness of their evening.

"I thought this was meant to be an archaeological trip Anna. Looks more like a holiday jaunt to me."

There was no mistaking the voice and accent of Rod McEwan, and she felt Martin's hand drop away as they turned in unison to face the unexpected, and unwelcome, apparition sitting at one of the tables. It was Anna who broke the bubble of silence that had absorbed them.

"Rod? How on Earth are you here – you should be in Wales."

"Not pleased to see your flatmate then Anna," came the reply.

She felt Martin's presence behind her as she said "Why are you here Rod?"

There was no mistaking the sarcastic edge to his voice as he answered.

"Just had to tell you the news that my little Welsh adventure has managed to uncover positive signs that Maxentius Gavius Corvinus established a fortified stronghold as far West as Anglesey, and so the XXVth Legion almost certainly did ship over to Ireland as has long been theorised. We've discovered what looks to be a huge fortified camp that's going to take some years to fully uncover."

The archaeologist came to the fore regardless of the sudden distaste with which she found herself viewing her university colleague's appearance.

"Wow, that's a major discovery Rod, well done. It looks as if all the pushing you did to convince the Uni to examine the Welsh site has paid off big time. But I don't see why you didn't just text or email me."

The red haired Scot had, from the moment of his uninvited entry into their evening, contrived to ignore Martins existence, and he looked at her without replying for several seconds, before saying "The dig has been granted additional finance from the Welsh Tourist Board, and Channel 4 is also putting up a big chunk of money so that we let them make a documentary about the whole project. Carson who was originally in overall charge has had a heart attack, and I've been made project leader with the freedom to take on extra staff. I want you Anna."

This last comment produced an audible snort from Price who without reference to Anna stepped past her and eased himself into a chair at the vacant adjacent table. He lounged back and despite his drooping eyelids Anna immediately recognised the misleading pose. She swallowed as she tried to ignore the set facial expression and, fighting the rising feeling of panic, thought for a few seconds, considering her reply carefully, before saying "It's kind of you Rod, very kind in fact, but I don't think I can accept."

"You mean you would rather stay on with this pointless treasure hunt than be involved in really meaningful archaeology?" Still no acknowledgement of Martin's existence.

"I want to see out this Sarony business Rod." She took a pace forward and heard the metal of the chair scrape on the terrace paving as she sat down to face him. "Both you and I know that if I were to decamp to Wales with you, then it would be sending out signals that on a personal level would be completely wrong."

Apparently unconscious of just how dangerously he was living, McEwan threw a contemptuous glance towards Martin, then turning back to face Anna resumed his argument.

"I'm talking archaeology Anna, but of course who knows how feelings could develop. We've been living under the same roof for months and it's only since this Sarony nonsense came up that things have changed."

"You may think you are talking archaeology Rod, but I know from recent experience that you are interested in a lot more than that, and frankly I'm not. Things, as you call them, were never more than platonic and will certainly never develop in the way you hope, at least from my standpoint."

Damn it! Couldn't he see that she was trying to put him off as diplomatically as possible? Instead of simply telling the little creep to get lost, she sat transfixed by the fear that Martin's silent presence could be transformed into something more intrusive should she somehow provoke the hot tempered Scot by humiliating him in front of a man he detested.

Undaunted, McEwan persisted. "You'd rather be supernumerary in the department would you? You do realise that Smithson-Hunt is going to channel all available resources into Wales? You will just be left answering the phones and making the coffee."

He smiled, and as he tossed another swift glance at Martin's motionless figure it crossed her mind that he was taking the whole matter of her open rejection of him a little too well. He picked up the glass he had been drinking from and, with another sideways glance at Price, said in an exaggerated change of tone. "Oh yes, I knew there was something else. Whilst you have been swanning around out here you may be interested to know that your excuse for clearing off to France for a romantic holiday at the Uni's expense was demolished due to storm damage back in Grantfield. Last week the top of St Bertha's bell tower was hit by lightning which dislodged a dirty great chunk of masonry and guess what?"

He paused theatrically, took another slow sip from his glass and smirked at Price who sat impassively watching him.

"Oh please God don't let him push too hard," she offered the silent payer having noticed Martin shift position slightly at McEwan's reference to a 'romantic holiday'. McEwan ploughed remorselessly onwards.

"No takers I see, never mind, I'll enlighten you anyway. Gravity had its way and said chunk plummeted one hundred feet and smashed through the grave of Chretien de Sarony and his lady wife. When they began tidying up the mess the following morning they found not only the mortal remains of the happy couple but also a small lead box containing a parchment. Thought you'd be interested so I've brought a translation with me." He fished in the inside pocket of his jacket saying "Here we are, let me read it for you:

'I Chretien de Sarony - etc etc um, here we go - *confess that having lost forever the treasure that occupied every waking and sleeping moment of my thoughts on my weary journey from Frosinone I now lay to rest my beloved wife Mathilde Hermione who has filled my years in England with what joy I now have found in in the service of the English King. I have never truly recovered from having the greatest wealth imaginable snatched from me within sight of the safety of my home and hope my feeble efforts have, dear wife, given you some small recompense for your devotion to one incapable of providing the love you had the right to expect.'*

His wife died before him as you know and it looks as if he had this little item buried with her. So you see it seems that the treasure is long gone, in fact it never quite made it back to Sarony."

He tossed the sheet of paper contemptuously onto the table and sat back with a smile. "How does my offer look now Anna?"

She bit nervously at her lip as she picked up the printed sheet of Grantfield University headed paper and scanned its message. "What does The Professor have to say?"

"Oh he agrees with me," replied McEwan airily. "Your little Sarony project is dead in the water. I'm flying back tomorrow, why not come with me? Price here can follow on and give the owner of Chateau Sarony the bad news that he's not sitting on a king's ransom buried by Chretien."

Anna felt her body tense as Price moved his chair, so that it joined the others at the small table, and spoke for the first time. "Did the Uni pay for you to fly out here McEwan?"

"None of your business Price, Anna and I are actually employed by Grantfield. You're just one of Smithson-Hunt's old pals that he's helping out because he feels sorry for you now mummy isn't around to look after her little boy."

Anna felt panic grip her as she saw Martin Price stiffen at the reference to his mother's death. She half rose from her chair as Price leaned forward and addressed his adversary, but his voice was low and without any trace of anger

"You paid for the flight yourself didn't you? This isn't about your Welsh project at all is it? You just want to play the hero in front of Anna and gloat about the Sarony treasure being a myth. Well McEwan, if Anna decides to throw in her lot with you that's entirely her decision, because contrary to your interpretation of the situation we are booked into single rooms. Whatever you thought you saw when we were walking back just now was nothing more than two colleagues sharing a moment of pleasure in pleasant surroundings."

And with those calm and controlled words Anna's beautiful new world was shattered into tiny smithereens. He rose and with a simple "Goodnight Anna" headed for his room.

She sat rooted to her seat wondering how within the space of half an hour an idyllic evening had been miraculously transformed into a nightmare. Moments later she also rose and without another word to Rod McEwan made her way into the hotel.

The victor was left alone to contemplate the now deserted field of battle and savour the fruits of his labours.

Chapter 16 - Colmierre

She slept badly and the lengthy shower did nothing to raise the despondency that had enveloped her from the moment Rod had made his poisonous appearance. Martin was already at the table and gave her a wave as she collected her coffee from the buffet. What she had begun to think of as the 'old Anna' suddenly made an appearance as she took her seat.

"Thanks for leaving me with Rod last night," she snapped.

He looked evenly at her with no trace of anger and said "It was for the best. Throwing The Rodent off the terrace into the rhododendrons would have been enormously satisfying, but it wouldn't have achieved anything would it?"

She noted the reversion to his insulting name for McEwan but couldn't somehow feel any urge to protest.

"It was better if I made myself scarce, I don't really want you to remember me as some sort of over aggressive bully. This was how it all started wasn't it, me letting McEwan needle me? On that occasion it was just chance, and I was off balance, but last night the little rat was doing it deliberately."

The words 'remember me' chilled her but before she could react he carried on.

"More to the point, you were suddenly put under a lot of unfair pressure last night, although McEwan is right about the Sarony affair. It's hardly real archaeology at all, more a glorified treasure hunt. Tying any career decision to it would be crazy, particularly in view of that letter from Chretien. You should make whatever you feel is the best decision for your own future, my future's already assured thanks to Armand's wealth. If you want to gain some breathing space don't feel obliged to stay. You can head for home right away if you like."

She silently shook her head feeling an enormous loneliness descend on her. She was suddenly on the outside looking in with the Welsh dig going ahead without her involvement, and the Sarony project at an end. She sat dumbly staring at her coffee as Price watched the golden head drooping disconsolately over her untouched breakfast, looking for all the world like a small child who has just received a severe telling off. When he spoke again it was with a less brash tone and the words were carefully chosen.

"OK, then let's get our things together and check out. We can finish our Sarony trip as planned. Chretien saw it through to the end and we can do the same. Perhaps we'll look in on Colmierre as planned and then get back to the chateau. I'd like to write up a diary of our trip which will at least tidy up things at this end. Then why don't you chill out at Sarony for a couple of days or so? Contrary to what The Rodent thinks, you aren't costing the Uni a penny above your usual wages so you can take a couple of days at least. In fact, rather than drag you back home in the Land Rover I'll buy you a nice comfy air flight, I want to look in on Bertrand and Emilie in any case, and I don't imagine a Land Rover trip to Calais will bring back happy memories for you."

She swallowed and realised that whatever might have evolved from their trip, not to mention last night's walk in the gardens, had been consigned to never-never land and they were back to affable colleague status. "OK," she agreed, "that would be nice, but what will you do now, after Calais that is?"

"Oh I'll be fine, just accelerate my plans a little. When I get back I'll look in on Smiffy at the Uni and have a de-briefing session, in fact you will be back a couple of days before me so if you are free perhaps we can all grab some lunch?"

She nodded miserably.

"Then I'll tie up a few loose ends and head back here to Sarony for the rest of the summer. I need to think about what to do with Orville Terrace, but thinking about it, you could do me an enormous favour."

"In what way?"

"Well I don't reckon you want to flat-share with The Rodent for much longer, so why not move into Orville Terrace? Popular des-res for a single girl, no riotous parties allowed of course, but you could simply house-sit for me while I'm here in Sarony, and if you wanted to pop back over here as my guest for a few days in sunny France then you would be very welcome."

A small spark ignited a flicker of hope amidst the burnt and blackened remains of yesterday's happiness.

"I – I don't know what to say Martin, that would be, well, wonderful. I could give some thought to my own future as well, as it looks as if it's all going a bit pear shaped at the Uni."

"Fine, settled then. No reason not to stay in touch is there."

The hiss of the snuffed out spark echoed in her head as he continued.

"Now let's head for Colmierre, and don't worry about The Rodent, he caught a very early flight – I checked with the desk."

"Why?"

"Why what?"

"Why did you check with the desk about The, er, Rode.., er, Rod?"

"I was going to ensure that he didn't get the opportunity to upset you again. You've looked like death warmed up ever since he surfaced."

And as they headed for reception she silently thanked God for at least balancing the books to a small extent.

Although larger than Sarony, Colmierre was still no more than a very small town and when they arrived Martin immediately steered them to the local church. It was, he explained, one of the few places that Chretien de Sarony could be identified as having stopped off at. "Look here" he said as he directed her to an inscribed stone set in the wall on the right hand side of the nave. "You'll have to translate," she said.

"Of course, well in a nutshell it says that due to a generous gift by Chretien on 31st May 1483 when he visited the parish it was possible for a new pulpit to be ordered and erected. In addition the church was pleased to bless the shrine that Chretien caused to be built on the road to Sarony in humble thanks for his safe return from the wars."

"Oh, I see." She half turned away from the wall then stopped, frowned, and turned back. Martin looked at her quizzically and waited as she stared vacantly at him for a moment before saying

"Seems a bit contradictory doesn't it?"

"Contradictory? How do you mean?"

She didn't answer immediately but instead began rummaging in the various pockets of her jeans. Martin waited patiently, enjoying the gyrations and wriggles that were performed in the urgent quest for whatever she had secreted within the tight fitting material.

She caught sight of the leer on his face as her fingers finally located the object of her search and turned her back on him. He heard the rustle of paper and then she said "Well, I've still got that bit of paper Rod threw at me last night."

"Good, how about turning round?"

She did so, glared at his still grinning face, and dropped her eyes to the sheet of paper.

"According to that bit of parchment the treasure was taken from him, um let's see, ah yes 'in sight of home' so there must have been some sort of conflict because someone like Chretien isn't going to lug his loot all the way from Italy and meekly hand it over without a fight is he?"

He nodded "Agreed."

She took a step to her left and pointed to the church wall.

"But according to your translation, here he is at Colmierre full of the joys of spring, so he must have still had his loot with him. You pointed out to me that little wayside shrine not long after we crossed the bridge on our way out. That's the shrine this stone mentions isn't it?"

"Yes that's right."

"So Martin, can we go and take a look at it now? It's on our way back and I'd like to see it, you said it's a bit of a landmark locally."

It was only a matter of minutes before they were standing at the roadside next to the little shrine. On the other side of the road, and a few yards south, stood an old country inn that Martin indicated with a sweep of his hand "According to local legend, Chretien stopped here at the inn and gave the landlord enough gold to pay for the pulpit down at the church in Colmierre and this shrine."

"There's an inscription on the shrine Martin – can you translate it?"

"Simple – it says *'With thanks to God for a safe return and his blessing on all travellers who offer a prayer at this place.'* Standard stuff really, you've probably noticed quite a few of these little shrines dotted around. In those days a long journey was a hazardous event."

"Look Martin, I'm no big expert on these things but it doesn't seem to make much sense to me."

"What's the problem?"

"Well you were a soldier weren't you, and presumably the general commonsense part of soldiering hasn't changed that much, even across several centuries?"

He shrugged and said "Go on."

"Exactly how close to the chateau are we Martin?"

He looked northwards along the line of the road which disappeared around the bend ahead.

"Sarony is only a couple of kilometres away, around the bend and across the bridge."

She turned and followed his gaze, hands on hips, suddenly confident.

"So why choose to attack a heavily armed fighting man at a point so close to Colmierre village and only a stone's throw from the victim's home ground? What sort of thinking is that, or am I missing something only a soldier would see?"

There was an unimaginably long pause as Martin stared intently at her, then he looked both up and down the road before saying: "Of course Anna, it's that parchment isn't it? I've hardly given it a second thought since McEwan read it to us."

He looked again at the rocky, almost sheer hillsides that bounded the road as it gradually ascended from Colmierre towards the hidden bridge.

"The terrain here is no place for an ambush. The parchment throws a whole new light onto what happened. It must mean that when Chretien was relieved of his loot it happened *between* here and Sarony, and once across the bridge in those days you would have been on Sarony property. You are right, between Colmierre and the chateau is a bonkers place to make such an assault, but if that's what happened then the only likely place is the bridge, but that doesn't make sense either."

"Why not Martin, I'm not a soldier remember?"

For the first time since they had walked back through the gardens at Poligny he touched her as he patted her upper arm saying,

"Come on, next stop is the bridge."

They drove across the bridge and again parked on the Northern side before walking back and tucking themselves into the central balcony that faced down the river valley towards the distant fields. He turned so that he faced inwards and with a sweep of his arm indicated the deserted road.

"You used the word 'commonsense' a few minutes ago, and you are dead right. It's not a matter of soldiering, just looking at the facts. Let's say our man and his cargo are on the bridge and, although a wooden structure, it was probably not much different in size to the stone one we are standing on now. As you can see, it's really not very wide, and that old bridge probably didn't have the walkways and balconies that this one's got.

Now you would attack from the front when he was in the middle so even though he can see you coming there is no way he can back up an ox-cart fast enough to escape. You've got him nicely trapped and you don't even have to charge straight into the attack. You can stand off and ask him to surrender because, assuming you've got him outnumbered, he's stuck with nowhere to go."

Anna shaded her eyes as she scanned the bridge in both directions before asking,

"Would an attack from the Colmierre direction not also work?"

"Well you could attack from the South but a number of armed men would be seen passing through Colmierre, and also coming past the inn, and if from the South then why not before he even got as far as Colmierre? We passed through a number of more suitable ambush sites on our way from Poligny. No, commonsense says that once past Colmierre then the bridge is the only suitable place. We also know that when he left the inn Chretien handed the innkeeper some gold to pay for the shrine, and so it wasn't just a matter of being attacked North of Colmierre, we can shave a couple of kilometres off and say with some certainty that the attack must have occurred North of the old inn."

"But in that case Martin you are saying that they must have attacked from, and then withdrawn to, Sarony property?"

"That's what it looks like, and it could well be that the people in Colmierre were none the wiser for quite some time."

Anna leaned back, her elbows resting on the curved parapet of the balcony and pursed her lips before saying, "But that begs a very interesting question which is how on Earth could they have got away?"

He nodded and said "Yes it's all very odd isn't it. We know that if they did actually jump Chretien on the bridge, then they could have dumped him and any men he had with him over the side and into the river below. They may then have had a chance of escaping with the treasure via Sarony land, but Chretien was a warrior, he would have died fighting them, and we know he didn't die. In fact we know that he took an active part in the Battle of Bosworth in England just a couple of years later."

"But we also know that he lost the treasure 'within sight of home' Martin, and that seems to me to indicate only one possibility."

"That the treasure went over the side of the bridge?"

"Exactly."

"To what purpose? Do you really imagine he had some sort of divine revelation and chucked a ton of gold over the side? More to the point, given the quantity, it would have taken a long period of quite hard physical effort to do something like that. Heavy metal in the traditional sense isn't going to just blow around in the wind, its going to pretty well stay put and even in a sparsely populated area somebody is going to come across it eventually, and there has never been a sniff of it across all these years."

"Could it still be in the river?"

He shook his head, "I'm afraid not, over the years various people have associated the name of the bridge with the Sarony Treasure legend, investigated the river, and drawn a complete blank."

As they walked back to the car Martin said,

"Anna, you don't think that little creep made up this parchment story just to wind us up do you?"

"No Martin, that's beyond even Rod's imagination, but you can always give your friend Smiffy a call can't you."

He nodded "Yes, I suppose so. I think that we are just going to have to resign ourselves to the fact that somehow Chretien lost the treasure five hundred years ago and we never are likely to find out the circumstances. Come on, I phoned Marcel earlier and we should have some good food and civilised surroundings to greet us at the chateau."

Chapter 17 - A Wren

The gates of Chateau Sarony slowly opened inwards in response to the remote reader installed in the X3. Martin had made another call to Marcel as they left the bridge, and the elderly couple were at the door of their cottage waving cheerfully as the X3 trundled past and headed for the main house.

Henrietta sighed "What do you think, is that one for Marti?"

Her husband did his usual impression of a typical Frenchman by shrugging, and at the same time pursing his lips and raising the bushy grey eyebrows. "Who knows? Marti is careful with his women."

"Huh, you mean like that tart at Fleurie?"

"Come now 'Etta, Monique may once have been a tart, but not now. She is a credit to the village, and Marti thinks the world of her."

His wife patted his arm "I know Marcel, it just makes me wild to know that the owner of Chateau Sarony has no woman in his life other than Monique, although this blonde one looks very nice. Have you seen anything to make you think that they, well, you know?"

"No 'Etta and you know as well as I do that they have separate rooms. He even told us when they arrived the other day that she is only a person from this work he is now doing."

As predicted, the kitchen was amply stocked with food, and the bedrooms had been re-equipped with freshly laundered sheets and fresh flowers taken from the garden. When Anna padded back downstairs in her shorts and halter neck T-shirt she found Martin on the garden terrace listening to birdsong, toasting himself gently in the sun, and already part way through a glass of white wine. If he had noticed her revealing attire he gave no sign.

"Help yourself," he said indicating the ice bucket that nestled in the shade.

She stood for a moment feeling the warmth of the flagstones caressing her bare feet and the rays of the sun washing the warmth across her body. Lost in a moment of undiluted pleasure she gazed out across the countryside and without thinking said "Oh it's so good to be home."

For Martin the minutes that had passed since her arrival on the terrace had been the most enjoyable since before the death of his mother. Ex- soldier that he was, he was quick to appreciate a position of strategic value. Having seated himself with his back to the countryside he was able to lounge, glass in hand and view the entire length of the chateau kitchen. Through half closed eyes he had watched her as she entered from the far end and walked unhurriedly towards where he was seated outside the appropriately named French windows. Feigned insouciance masked his complete focus on the blond pony tail, the red T-shirt, and the long legs protruding from the small white shorts. He continued to regard her in silence as the realisation of what she had just said caused her to flush bright crimson and stammer.

"Wh-what I-I m-meant was. Oh sod it, you know what I meant," and she hastily poured herself some wine and stood cradling her elbow in the palm of her other hand without meeting his eyes.

He was loath to say anything that would interrupt his contemplation of her as she stood facing out over the garden, but finally had to rejoin the rest of the world if only to ease her feelings.

"No need to feel embarrassed, it's been a long, frustrating, and not entirely happy experience, and I'm as pleased to get back here as you. It's been a long time since the old place had a woman call it home. My ex-wife never came here, and heaven knows who the last mistress of Sarony was."

His cheerful tone blew away her awkwardness. She gratefully eased herself into a chair, realised her glass was empty and helped herself to a refill as he pushed a tray of salad and cold meat towards her.

"It's nice to relax after a journey, and talking of home, don't forget what I said about Orville Terrace, I don't want rent, and don't be in a rush to leave. I expect to spend the foreseeable future here, and if I did need to stay in Grantfield I'm sure you could put up with me roosting in one of the spare rooms for a day or two, couldn't you?"

"Yes, I would like to get away from Rod and his flat as soon as possible. I will take up your offer but, after this morning's discussion, is the Sarony project definitely at an end?"

He scratched his chin and said slowly "We-ell, we can spend some time on a complete review if you like. I want to write up a diary of our trip from our notes and things, so that would be a good opportunity to see if there is any mileage in spending more time."

"That's settled then" answered Anna as she helped herself to another glass of wine, "then I can clear off out of your way to Grantfield."

As she spoke she noticed a familiar figure appear on the far side of the garden and stoop to wield secateurs in combat with the rose bushes. "I hope Marcel and his wife don't believe that our trip was just an excuse for the sort of thing that Rod has obviously been thinking." She took another long swallow of the wonderfully cold liquid.

"I don't see why they should" he responded.

She was just thinking how strange it was that her glass was nearly empty again when she realised a response was required.

"No reason really, just that now he can see us lazing around together just like... oh bugger I've nearly done it again haven't I?"

"Done what?" He enquired innocently?

"Hang on, just having my second."

"Second?"

"Nice this wine. Now what did you say?"

"You said you had nearly done it again."

"Did I? Oh yes I did didn't I. Yes well what I meant was..." She paused to gather her thoughts then added "well, yes, I nearly said something about us acting like a proper couple and that was silly because I'd already called this place home, and it isn't is it?"

"Well I think of it as home" he said.

"Ah that's what I mean" she said wondering why she seemed to be feeling hotter even though the sun had moved off her. She helped herself to another glass of wine as she warmed to her theme. "Yes that's my point. You're home so you'd better watch out or tongues will wag won't they?"

"Will they?"

God, was he being intentionally dim?

" 'Course they will. Bound to. Small place like this. Her expressively waving arm neatly decapitated a rose that 'Etta had thoughtfully placed on the table earlier.

He looked at the rose, then back at her as she added "I mean to say, first you put up one fallen woman in an auberge in France and now…" he quickly interrupted by saying:

"…and now a second one both here and in Grantfield? Ta-da, may I present Anna Freemont who can't make up her mind whether she is a needy spinster or a fallen woman."

For some reason Anna found this comment hilarious and Martin who had been watching her get slowly pickled said "You do realise that you are completely pissed don't you?"

"Don't be rid, rid. Don't be silly. Look, bottle's empty."

She rose to her feet and to prove her point walked perfectly steadily over to the fridge. Unfortunately the whole affect was spoilt when she bumped into it and apologised. Martin exploded with laughter as she wrestled the door open and unsteadily withdrew a fresh bottle. With a glass in one hand and a bottle in the other it took Anna some seconds to figure out that the best way to close the fridge door was to lean back against it. "Oh God" she thought as she wobbled backwards, but Martin's continuing hilarity brought on a fit of the giggles and for a while even Marcel at the other end of the garden could hear the merriment.

The laughter when it died was replaced by the sound of a wren in one of the trees shouting at them to be quiet.

As Anna finally escaped from the clutches of the fridge she heard a voice sounding uncannily like her own say,

"I can't drink all of this by myself Martin. Don't forget to bring your glass up with you," and she made her way unsteadily back through the kitchen and along the passageway to the main stairs.

Chapter 18 - Library

Rather like a transatlantic flight, the whole lopsided pattern of the day left them feeling disorientated. Intense physical exercise combined with helpful quantities of wine also has a tendency to induce drowsiness and so when they finally tottered back downstairs, the summer's evening was well advanced and sleep was something neither of them felt inclined to accept. On the contrary, they were both fully awake, ravenously hungry and, if truth were told, anticipating a return match at an early date. Swathed in a gown supplied by Martin, Anna's old adversary - the fridge - proved no match for their combined assault and swiftly capitulated without a struggle. They carried their prizes to the library and were sitting gorging themselves when Anna's phone chirruped. She sprinted out to the hall and returned frantically rummaging in the handbag that she had carelessly dropped when they had arrived earlier.

Having finally located the phone and heedless of a number of items that were scattered onto the floor by her efforts she stared for a moment at the handset, and muttered "Bollocks" before bending to retrieve the fallout.

"Bad news?"

"Bad odour more like, it's a text from Rod telling me the offer is still open."

"Tell him you're busy auditioning for the Playboy Calendar."

"What? Oh, oops sorry." She made a show of rearranging the dressing gown.

"Don't apologise, I've never been so entertained by a girl looking through her handbag. Don't forget that bit of paper over there. Oh dear, these dressing gowns must be the dodgy French variety."

She pulled a face, retrieved the crumpled paper and was about to toss it into the waste-bin by the desk when she stopped, stared and then said "Martin, take a look at this."

Still in play mode his response of "I've eyes for nothing else," earned him a punch on the shoulder.

"No, behave yourself and look. I've just noticed something strange." She thrust the headed sheet of Grantfield University paper under his nose and jabbed her finger at the printed words *Mathilde Hermione*.

Baffled, he stared at the notepaper and finally gave up with a shake of the head saying "Sorry my love but you've got me. What am I supposed to see?"

"Her name, or rather names, look what do you see?"

"Mathilde Hermione."

She looked at him, sighed and said. "Instead of eyeing innocently displayed female flesh why not be a good boy and go and look at the picture of the happy family at the top of the stairs, go on shoo."

"I'm impressed," were his first words as he re-entered the library "Mathilde Eugenie" is what it says.

"Do you think it means anything?"

"Probably more sloppy work by our friend Rod, a bit like that survey. Still let's see what Smiffy has to say shall we? He's a bit of a late owl"

Professor Smithson-Hunt seemed pleased to receive the call and, after giving him a brief resume of the Italian trip, Martin let him cover the recent events at St Bertha's without interrupting:

"Well as you can imagine Martin, that great chunk of masonry was really travelling by the time it hit terra-firma, and it so happened that the terra in question was not quite so – ah – firma as it might have been. It went straight through and smashed into the Sarony Vault below and that's how we found that parchment."

"It's the genuine article then Smiffy?"

"So far as we can tell old boy it's absolutely genuine. Sorry to say that combined with young McEwan's Welsh adventure it means I've got to pull the plug on your Sarony jaunt. Any idea when we can have our Miss Freemont back?"

"Oh, it'll be a few days yet Smiffy, we've only just got back ourselves. One thing though – have you got a copy of the parchment to hand?"

"I can email you a photo old boy, I'm in my study at home now and if I can remember how to work this bloody machine, let's see, ah yes. OK it's either on it's way to you or I'm going to have a man with a pizza appearing shortly. By the way, who told you about this business?"

"McEwan?"

"Oh yes of course, I gather that he and Anna Freemont are quite close, at least that's what he said. I've agreed that she can be his number two in Wales if she wants to – course of true love and all that. You heard about Carson?"

"Yes, from the same source. Well thanks Smiffy, it looks like the Sarony thing is a dead duck and I'll get Anna to contact you as soon as she makes her decision."

He dropped the phone onto the settee and looked at her, "Apparently McEwan has given Smiffy the impression that you and he are about one step short of the wedding bells. I thought it best if I stayed out of it and let you tell him what the true story is. Let's see if that email has arrived shall we?"

As they stood shoulder to shoulder in front of the PC she said. "Just now, when I was showing you the piece of paper that Rod brought you called me 'my love'."

"Did I?"

"Yes."

"Well, I must have meant it mustn't I. Aha here's the email."

As he opened the emailed attachment she said "For once Rod got it right – 'Mathilde Hermione' is what it says. So do we assume that the picture is wrong?"

"My first reaction would be to say yes, but I do wonder whether this now links up with that comment of Armand's about his wife. Where's my note book? Come on eagle-eyes where is it? Oh thanks" He took the book that she had unearthed from beneath the food tray and flicked through the pages.

"Here we are:

'Why didn't wife and child go to England?'

There may be no trace of the boy, but that comment seemed to contradict irrefutable evidence to the contrary so far as the wife is concerned. When we talked about it a week or so ago we agreed it was baffling."

Anna pursed her lips and said "It still does contradict the facts, doesn't it?"

"I'm wondering if it does. Armand only ever dealt in facts and I wonder if what we have is an *apparent* contradiction rather than a real one. Armand was so precise, and making an erroneous statement in his notes when he only had to look in the church at Grantfield, is just not the sort of sloppy schoolboy error he would make. Now we have the parchment telling us that the wife's name differs from what a family portrait states.

181

Supposing nothing is wrong and it's all correct, that would leave only one explanation wouldn't it?"

She stood thinking for a moment before answering,

"Two different women?"

"Bingo Anna. Thanks to you I think that we have found out something that Armand had already worked out. Chretien either remarried, or took a mistress who had an identical Christian name to his wife in the picture. I'd favour the mistress answer, his wife in all but name. He never did go back to France did he? Instead, he stayed in service with Henry here in England, and if he wasn't actually married to Mathilde Hermione who would know, or even care for that matter?"

"Even so Martin, although we seem to have resolved two out of the three notes that Armand made, I don't see what good it does. We are still stranded at the same point we reached yesterday."

"Admittedly it's probably purely academic now, but the fact is that when we started, the treasure was still not fully acknowledged as being factual rather than mythical. Now we know that it really did exist. When we started, it's whereabouts was unknown, that is still the case, but we now know that it was somehow pinched from Chretien in this general area, and that he seems to have made no effort to regain it. He simply throws his hat in the ring with Henry Tudor and buggers off to England."

"So where do we go from here?"

"That's up to you really. Smiffy asked me when he could expect you back, and you have got a career to think about. We can squeeze a few more days out of this, maybe a week but, sooner rather than later, you have to decide whether you are going to stay at Grantfield Uni. That decision could be influenced by whether we make further progress whilst you are here couldn't it? My feeling is that we should review all of our notes, write up our trip, and see if we can throw any further light on the subject."

"OK, I'm happy with that."

"Good, we can start in earnest tomorrow."

"And what do we do between now and then?" She posed the question as she backed towards the library door.

Chapter 19 - Chapel

All things considered, they enjoyed breakfast together at a not unreasonable time. Neither of them had been aware of Marcel lurking beneath Martin's bedroom window a couple of hours earlier before hastening off to report to Henrietta. As they finished stacking the dishwasher Martin straightened up, looked at Anna and said "Fit for work Miss Freemont?"

"Barely Mr Price, I seem to have woken up with bruises and marks in the places that nice girls don't even admit to possessing. You sir, are a brute!"

"That's a yes then?"

"OK, let's head for the library and get to work."

The fun and interest of the previous week of travel and then their more recent activities soon faded as they began to wade through the various reference books that remained stacked where Martin had placed them before their trip. When those sources were exhausted they ran some equally unprofitable lines of enquiry via the internet before Martin settled to writing up the diary of their trip, with Anna prompting him, and amusing herself by sniping at his ponderous keyboard skills.

By agreement they did not include any reference to McEwan's visit and simply referred to having discovered the news about the parchment without specifying the source. It was two days later, having re-read and corrected their notes, that the glum truth became apparent. They still seemed to be at a dead end, and it was again Anna who suggested a new line of enquiry when she said that they now ought to focus their attention on the mystery of the missing child.

"I've taken the liberty this past few days Martin, of looking around the whole of the chateau."

"I wondered where you kept disappearing off to."

"Your typing speed of one word per minute was making me dizzy so I needed to take a break occasionally."

"Oh ha-ha.

"Thought I was just being nosy did you?"

He shrugged "I did think it was a bit odd, but there are a lot of things I don't know about you, I mean you could be a frustrated estate agent couldn't you."

"I'm ignoring your childish attempts to provoke me and have to inform you that, with the exception of the family portrait, I cannot find a single trace in either the house or the grounds of either Mathilde Eugenie or her son. Not that I really expected to find anything in the house."

"So you were just being nosy."

"If you don't shut up I won't tell you about the unusual fact that I did find, something that I believe could prove interesting."

Martin had laid to one side his bantering manner and was now listening earnestly to what she was saying, "Go on" he encouraged.

The unsmiling concentration that she had once found disconcerting now stimulated her, and she plunged ahead.

"At first I drew a complete blank with the house itself, and then having worked my way round the grounds my initial thought was that the same applied. But after giving it a lot of careful consideration I realised that there is something peculiar that bears further examination."

"Something in the grounds you say?"

"Yes, and strange as it may sound, it's not the absence of something we are looking for that has made me think, but the absence of something we are not looking for."

"Well now I am confused. What aren't we looking for that is missing, but may be relevant to what we are looking for?"

"Chretien's ancestors."

"What have they got to do with all of this?"

"Nothing directly, but although there is a family graveyard over in the northwest corner behind that line of trees that hides it from sight of the house, there are no graves or vaults there that are dated before 1505."

"What's significant about 1505?"

"Nothing, that just happens to be the earliest dated burial and could well refer to the guy who inherited from Chretien. But what I am saying is, there is nothing earlier, despite the chateau having been built in something like 1320."

"So where are they?"

"That's what I'm asking Martin. Surely there would have been a burial ground or a family vault?"

"Yes of course there would, and the most likely place would have been below the chapel."

"Supposing the chapel wasn't destroyed during Napoleonic times but a lot earlier, it would account for the dating of those burials above ground wouldn't it?"

"Sounds logical but unfortunately the sacking of the chapel is a documented historical event."

"Oh, I'd hoped it was just one of those rumours that had gained credence over a period of time. But wouldn't that mean we would expect to find much less above ground before late eighteenth century?"

He leaned back against the desk and thought. "That's right, but that means we've got two mysteries doesn't it. First of all where are the pre 1505 burials, and secondly why bury those later generations from 1505 to say 1800 above ground when there was a family vault available?"

"Could the pre 1505 ancestors be buried in the church down in the village?"

"No, that doesn't work because in Chretien's day there wasn't a village, it was just Sarony land. Even Auberge Fleurie wasn't built until sometime in the sixteenth century."

"But what about the people working on the land?"

"Sarony lands were extensive in those days and there were already established villages and hamlets. The villages had churches and so there was never any difficulty with burials for them."

"But Martin, this seems to make less sense the more we find out. If there was a perfectly good chapel at the chateau why would all of Chretien's descendants be buried elsewhere in the same grounds?"

"That's a very good question, why indeed if the chapel was still standing? Unless for some reason it couldn't be used."

"Could the building have become unsafe?"

"I suppose that's possible, but if so, why not fix it? I know Chretien's descendants were hopeless with money but they weren't that hard up."

"Do we know where the chapel once stood?"

"I don't know with any great accuracy, but I gather it was somewhere near to where the front gates are now sited. That wall wasn't erected until the mid - nineteenth century but I seem to recall Marcel telling me years ago that his cottage was built with the stones from the old chapel"

"The cottage isn't built on the chapel site is it?"

'I'm sure its not. Marcel once showed me some old architect's drawings and a ledger recording the costs of building the cottage, and I'm sure that's where I've got the idea of the old chapel location."

"The fact that they live in something built from a former religious building doesn't bother Marcel and his wife?"

"I don't think so, in any case when a church building falls into disuse they perform some form of ceremony to deconsecrate it and scare all the ghosties away."

Anna, who had been walking up and down the library, halted and suddenly clapped her hands together like an excited child.

"Of course, that's it Martin, you can't just go around burying bodies wherever you like, and until Napoleon's time France was a strongly religious country."

"I don't follow!"

"It's just come to me. What is the one thing they would have had to do to set up the burial site beyond the trees?"

"Um well, oh yes. They would have needed to have it consecrated wouldn't they?"

"Exactly, and so if we flip the coin over we might now infer a possible solution to our earlier question of was there something that stopped them from using the chapel. Something on religious rather than structural grounds would be more plausible wouldn't it? Perhaps the chapel couldn't be used because it had been, damn it what's the bloody word? Yes, desecrated, that's it, perhaps the chapel had been desecrated Martin."

"Impressive line of reasoning Anna, you're not just a pretty face are you?"

She grinned "I've been told I've got a nice bum as well."

He began to edge past her as he replied "True, but you've managed to talk out of the right end this time, ouch!"

She delivered a hefty punch to his shoulder.

"You're developing a penchant for physical violence Miss Freemont."

"It's the company I'm keeping, now get up those stairs if you know what's good for you."

The following day marked Anna's formal introduction to the Morane family as represented by Marcel and Henrietta, or 'Etta as she was generally known. It also marked Anna's decision to make a determined effort to learn French, as although the old couple were able to stumble along with their rarely used English, they automatically spoke to Martin in their mother tongue with the result that much of the conversation simply swirled about her. She was also less than convinced by Martin's protestations that his translations were accurate, particularly when a long interrogation by 'Etta resulted in her beaming at Anna and examining her from a variety of angles as if she was a museum exhibit. Martin's explanation that she was fascinated by Anna's tall, almost Nordic stature didn't entirely ring true. Shortly afterwards, she was sure she caught Marcel staring at her backside when he thought she was listening to his wife identifying the subjects in the line of family photographs standing proudly on the living room dresser.

They settled at the large dining table as 'Etta brought coffee and cake for them while Martin explained in English, for Anna's benefit, but with frequent lapses into rapid French, that they wanted to pinpoint the site of the old chapel. Marcel duly rolled out of the room and after a minute or two could be heard clumping around above their heads. This was followed by the sound of something heavy being dragged across the floor of the upper room. Shortly afterwards he triumphantly returned brandishing a roll of papers and a small leather bound book.

By the time they left the cottage they had a pretty accurate idea of where the chapel had once stood, and Marcel insisted on accompanying them to the site that was close to the main gates as Martin had thought. Anna volunteered to collect some marker poles from the Land Rover and soon returned to find Marcel and Martin in heated debate, with Marcel in particular performing a passable impression of a windmill as he shrugged and waved his way through his argument. Martin in contrast moved little, but frequently interjected a stream of words at a pace that, to Anna, sounded like an incomprehensible jet of criticism. "Will I ever get the hang of this bloody language?" she wondered as the two men suddenly recognised her reappearance and a couple of short sharp verbal missiles from Martin were followed by a shrug, and "Bon, d'accord" from Marcel.

Some form of procedure seemed to have been formulated because Marcel found four hefty stones and pinned the chapel plan to the ground. Martin then astounded her by reverting to English with "Anna, would you mind standing on my shoulders and climbing up onto the wall?"

"Onto the wall? Martin, it's about ten feet high."

"Nearer twelve feet actually, but once you are on my shoulders you will be able to reach up with your arms and pull yourself up."

She looked at him aghast, opened her mouth to protest, and closed it again as she realised that he was deadly serious. She reluctantly took hold of Marcel's outstretched hand to act as a steadying support. Martin braced himself with his back to the wall, and she lifted her foot and placed it on his interlinked fingers. Gripping his shoulder with her free hand, she pressed down with her raised leg and hauled herself upwards using Marcel's hand as a brace. Once she was positioned on Martin's shoulders it was a simple matter to grab hold of the upper edge of the wall and hang there for the few seconds it took for him to spin around, put his hands beneath her feet and heave upwards.

For one frightening moment she thought she would be catapulted clean over the wall and plunge headlong down on the other side. Her impetus suddenly slowed as Martin slackened his pressure and with her upper half flopping onto the wide parapet it was a simple matter to then ease herself fully onto the flat sun-warmed surface. Making a mental note to claim for the cost of new jeans and T-shirt from the University Site Expenses Fund she gave herself a half minute to settle her nerves before slowly getting to her feet and standing upright. It was only as she looked down at the grinning upturned faces of the two men below that it occurred to her to ask "Martin, just why the hell am I up here?"

"I always put my women on a pedestal. I've ordered a brunette for the other side of the gates."

"Bastard."

"OK, I'm going to try and mark out the chapel using the poles and tape by following Marcel's instructions as he reads the architect's drawing."

"How long ago was the chapel demolished?"

Another quick fire exchange took place between the two men before Martin answered,

"About 1836."

"Bloody hell, what exactly do I do?"

I want you to move back and forth on the wall and sing out if, from your superior height, you can see anything that's not obvious from ground level."

"OK" she answered doubtfully.

They started with the north-west corner on the side nearest to the wall which meant that Anna could gaze almost directly straight down on Martin as he walked slowly along in obedience to Marcel's shouted instructions. Marcel suddenly uttered a brief command and looking up he called "Anything?" But she only shook her head. He had begun to drive the metal pole into the grassy surface when, having crouched down and shielded her eyes with her hand, she hurriedly called out:

"Hang on," and slowly moved ahead of him in a series of crouching hops. When she finally halted she was able to focus on what seemed to be a change in the texture of the grass a few yards ahead of where Martin had first paused.

"I think you need to move forward some more, a few more paces so you are just below me. Yes, about there."

The next hour was filled with shouted conversations between the three of them as they endeavoured to mark out the chapel boundaries. They finally completed the task and although Anna spent a tiring hour capering back and forth along the top of the wall, she did feel that the resulting aching leg muscles and grubby clothing were worthwhile. When it was agreed that her aerial role had been fully exploited Martin backed against the wall and she eased herself down onto his shoulders. He slowly bent his knees and lowered her another half metre to enable her to hop easily to the ground.

"Something tells me you've done this sort of thing before," she said.

"Only with nice girls" he grinned.

"Was it useful?"

"You're a trooper Anna. Well done," was the response.

It was agreed that they would spend the rest of the day planning their next step. Marcel happily loaned the drawings and ledger to Martin and headed home for his afternoon nap.

Back in the library they sat and mulled over their options.

"Now that we've got an idea of the chapel site we have to establish where to start our search for the vault, and how far down we need to go before we hit pay dirt," said Martin. "Although by comparison to a church the chapel is small, we still need to determine where our best point of entry will be. I believe we should assume that the chapel entrance was centrally located in the narrow side facing west, purely because it would be logical if the existing driveway and approach road follow the same line as in medieval times."

"Any thoughts on the location of the vault?"

"I'm willing to take a bet that it was accessed via a set of steps in the ground by the outside rear wall. A small chapel like this would have needed to maximise its internal space for worship so a basement access from the outside would make complete sense. When a funeral service was finished the body could be carried back down the central aisle, out through the main entrance, and around to the rear access. If the bodies were encased in wooden coffins then easy access would be essential."

Anna nodded "So we should start by cutting a trench along the line of the rear wall?"

"Yes, that would be my approach, but unless the building game has changed I don't think its something we would want to tackle with hand tools, even if I could get Marcel to round up some likely lads from the village."

"Why will digging out the entrance prove difficult, always assuming it's where you think it is?"

"Because if you are a builder and have a nice handy hole, then you use it to take all the debris and rubbish. It saves you carting it off site.

"I don't see why the soldiers would bother with an unused chapel."

"The fact that the chapel probably hadn't been used for worship for several hundred years won't have impressed the citizen's soldiery. No doubt if the house was reasonably defended they would have chosen an easier target. Yobs are yobs whatever century they live in, and an undefended chapel would present the opportunity for a nice face-saving exercise in pointless destruction. So when Napoleon's boys trashed the interior, and fired the roof you would have been left with little more than a shell full of rubbish. By the time we get to 1836 my betting will be that the access area to the vault is half filled with junk anyway, and so in time honoured fashion the builders will have tidied up by dumping as much debris as possible into the access area, levelled the ground and that's it."

"That certainly sounds logical Martin. What makes you so sure?"

"These ledger entries from 1836 are very detailed but make no mention of any cost of cartage to remove rubbish from site. So what else would you do with it?"

"And so you anticipate a lot of stuff to dig out from the vault access."

"Yes, at least not just earth. Tiles, pieces of wooden rafter, bricks, which is why I suggest we take the trusty Land Rover back to England and collect my mate Mickey. I'm sure he'll enjoy a trip to France and I can show you how to operate a digger - a skill all lady archaeologists should possess in my opinion. Say a three day round trip, maybe four."

"I could go and see The Prof as well couldn't I?"

"It would be courteous to give him an update even though your days are numbered."

"Oh God, can you believe I'd forgotten about that?"

Chapter 20 - Marcel

"I wish we could have taken the X3," said Anna as they pulled away from Auberge Fleurie.

They had looked in briefly on Monique whom Martin wanted to see, having only spoken to her once or twice on his mobile since they left on their trip to Italy. Monique had been sitting on the patio with a cup of coffee and had watched as the English couple drew up in the Land Rover and made their way through the bar to join her. Anna couldn't repress a twinge of envy as she saw how at ease Monique was in Martin's company, but when the French girl embraced her and murmured "Tres bon Cherie" in her ear she knew that there was no envy behind the French girl's words.

"Yep, the X3 is certainly comfier but this is a good runabout and I don't have to worry about scratching the paintwork – also I don't have a tow-bar fitted to the X3."

"I've been wondering what I should say to The Prof when I see him."

"In what way?"

She fished carefully in her mind for the correct answer before saying. "If I'm not going to Wales, and I'm not, then I'll have to settle for second best until that project has finished and heaven knows when that might be. At present it just looks like admin in the department. It's not as if I've any great savings, and so I don't want to just hand in my notice without being more sure of my future, but I do think that I'll have to start looking around to see what else may be on offer."

"I see your point, and it's certain that the Sarony task won't last much more than a few more weeks at the most, at least that's how I see it."

She winced inwardly at his apparent unwillingness to talk in terms of their ongoing relationship, and as if reading her thoughts he added:

"This is something you have to decide for yourself without regard to what I may think, it's your career and you need to look at each of the options carefully, but I do have one suggestion."

"And that is?"

"Why not ask The Prof if you can have three months unpaid leave? That will take you way beyond our Sarony work and you can then relax either at Orville Terrace, or better still, here in France at the chateau. My original invitations were made before things, er, developed between us. Let everything gain a perspective, and I'm sure The Prof will be happy to get you back in the fold if you then decide that it's Grantfield Uni for you."

She was tempted to say the classic line 'what about us' but resisted the impulse. Things had moved swiftly since they had first arrived in France and, although she was now again bouncing along in the Land Rover, she knew that her entire life had changed for the better since that horrible outward journey.

"I may well take up that suggestion Martin. Now what are the plans for our visit to Grantfield?"

"I would like to say that we could spend a week at Orville Terrace, and I would take you to all the nicest restaurants and watch you put on at least a stone in weight. My intention though is for us to spend tonight at the house, then you have your meeting at 11.00 with Smiffy tomorrow while I hitch up the trailer and load Mickey. I pick you up at 12.30 and we head back to Dover. All things being equal we should be back at the chateau sometime during the evening if I put my foot down. Are you are happy to put up with that schedule."

"No stopping off to see Bertrand and Emilie?"

"Not this time, although I would like to see them. My friends are very important to me as you may have realised, but once I've got something moving I like to keep at it. To be honest I've thoroughly enjoyed myself out here on this silly treasure hunt, and instead of selling Mickey, I've decided that I'm going to keep him at the chateau."

"OK, I'm happy to make this a flying visit as you suggest, but if I get up at the crack of dawn tomorrow could I borrow the Land Rover and make a few trips to ferry my stuff over to Orville Terrace? I really don't want to spend any more time as Rod's flatmate."

"Fine, getting up early doesn't bother me. I'll give you a hand if you like, then if necessary you can always come back for a day or so once we've got this chapel business settled."

"You don't think it's likely that we will run into those people again, you know, the ones you dealt with in Calais?"

"I doubt it, in fact I rather suspect they will have been blacklisted as football hooligans. If so they will have trouble getting any of the ferry companies to accept them." He winked at her and added "Don't worry Anna, let's get this little jaunt out of the way and I'll teach you to handle Mickey, so if you end up without a job you can dig up the roads like me."

That prospect did not appeal to her in the least, and it was with some relief that she sat in Smithson-Hunt's study the following morning explaining her dilemma. He sat studying the young woman as he listened and gained the impression that there was something different about her. It was nothing he could precisely identify, just a perception that she was somehow indefinably changed from the person of a few weeks before.

"A three month break unpaid you say? Well, I don't think I will have too much trouble persuading the purse holders to go along with that. But are you sure you don't want to join up with young McEwan in Wales, I thought that you and he were um, sort of, well, a couple? At least that was the impression he gave me when he asked if I'd agree to you partnering him now that poor Carter is laid low, and you do live together don't you?"

"No Professor not in the sense you mean. It's true that we share a flat, but I'm his paying tenant and that is the full extent of our personal arrangements which I will in any event be terminating with effect from today. Rod McEwan has never been anything more than a colleague, and there is no chance of me agreeing to work as his subordinate."

"Alright Anna, but it could well be that this Welsh business will be the making of him, and if so, the powers that be will lean heavily on me to make him head of department in view of what they will see as your less than enthusiastic commitment. That's not my view I hasten to add, but circumstances seem to have conspired against you at this particular time, and McEwan has caught the eye having risen to the occasion following Carter's illness."

"I understand Professor." She rose to leave but he held up his hand to delay her exit saying:

"You haven't told me how this Sarony venture is going. Martin has left me a few cryptic messages, but I gather the news isn't very positive."

"No, not terribly. I'll let him put you fully in the picture, but it looks as if whatever we can achieve so far as the private chapel is concerned will probably prove a dead end, and then I think we will have to admit defeat. I know that Martin intends to bring you up to date as soon as we wrap up this particular line of enquiry."

By the time they drove into Sarony it was nearing 10 o'clock due to an accident on the road South of Calais and then a flat tyre. They had risen at 5 a.m. and spent several hours driving back and forth between McEwan's flat and Orville Terrace as they ferried Anna' belongings to one of the large guest bedrooms.

Although she knew that Rod was in Wales, it had still come as a relief to Anna to find that the flat was completely deserted. Her final task, as Martin waited in the Land Rover with the last load, was to leave a brief note informing her erstwhile landlord that she would not be returning, and that if he hadn't already found it, her key was on the doormat. She could not resist adding that she had felt it necessary to correct the impression of the professor that there had been some sort of romantic link between them.

Now they were both dog tired as Martin silently piloted the vehicle and it's trailer through the village, remarking only that Monique had closed early as they passed the darkened auberge.

They slept the sleep of the exhausted and having finally hauled themselves in a zombie like state of mental dysfunction out of bed, they embraced the revivifying properties of caffeine with slowly returning awareness.

"Will you be up for a quick course in digger driving, or would you prefer to leave the work for tomorrow?" Price ventured over his third cup.

"I didn't realise you were serious about that, but yes I'll give it a go. In fact the way things are at present I may well be able to use the additional skill - as you said the other day."

"I think that a girl should have, oh I wonder who that can be?"

This last comment came as a loud knocking on the front doors echoed through the hall. Anna helped herself to another slice of toast and, as she heard Martin unbolt and open the front door, the murmur of voices drifted through to her. She was sure that she recognised Marcel's voice and then Martin raised his voice but without her being able to make out his words although, from the pattern, it sounded as if he was firing a string of questions at the old man. Rapid footsteps sounded and she realised that Martin was running upstairs. Thoroughly mystified she rose and, gathering the dressing gown about her, stepped from the kitchen into the entrance hall where she saw Marcel standing just inside the doorway like some Gallic walrus, hands on hips. An object on the floor caught her eye and she recognised the heap of material as Martin's dressing gown. Perplexed, she called to Marcel who replied in his halting English.

"It is OK M'selle Anna, Marti will deal with it."

This oblique comment perplexed her even further, and a feeling of unease began to creep through her like a cold shadow.

"What will Martin deal with, what has happened?"

The Gallic shrug preceded the opening of the walrus mouth, but before Marcel could utter there came again the sound of running feet, this time booted, as Martin descended the long winding flight two at a time. Fully dressed in jeans T-shirt and denim jacket he carried in his right hand a large holdall, and she saw that he also had a rucksack slung over one shoulder. As his boots crashed onto the hall floor he hurled a further stream of French at Marcel, veered around Anna who had moved towards him and sped out through the front door.

An eerie feeling of déjà vu hit Anna as the incident on their first journey through Calais came back to mind with startling clarity. The peculiar feeling that although Martin seemed to be moving at superhuman speed, time was somehow slowed down and she could replay her memory as if in slow motion. She heard again the sharp crack of breaking bones and saw the tall Liverpudlian collapsing in a bloodied heap. Reaching out she supported herself on the end post of the balustrade as her knees suddenly turned to mush and felt as if they would give way. Marcel took two paces towards her, grabbed her other arm with his hand and murmured.

"Do not worry, Marti will know what to do."

The words were intended as a comfort, but did no better than heighten the sinister feeling of apprehension that was further magnified by the sound of the Land Rover engine being started with a screeching roar and the rattle of flying shingle as it accelerated along the drive. She took a deep breath and tried to shake from her mind the picture of Martin's face as he had careered around her moments before. She could never before recall being so scared as she had been at that moment when the eyes of the man she had been eating toast and coffee with only minutes earlier gazed through her into some far distant realm with an intensity that could only be described as terrifying. Every other muscle and angle of his face was set like immovable stone from which those eyes, that could light up and glint with mischief and laughter, had frozen her words in her throat as he charged past. She let Marcel shepherd her back to the confines of the kitchen and watched as he fetched himself a coffee cup, poured into it the dark liquid and proceeded to tell her in his slow eccentric English what had caused the disintegration of the peaceful day.

Chapter 21 - Monday

When Marcel had left, Anna sat quietly pondering her next course of action. She could of course panic, simply pack her bags, call a taxi and head for Grantfield. Once there she would soon find herself a flat, move her belongings out of Orville Terrace and settle back into her life at the University until something better came along. She discarded the Dunkirk option without more than a momentary hesitation and, resisting the temptation to shed tears, reviewed her other possible courses of action.

She could sit tight where she was at the chateau and wait for Martin to return or call, or in the worst case scenario receive a call from a third party. She could head for the Morane cottage and seek refuge in the comforting words of Marcel and 'Etta who would no doubt be happy to take care of 'Marti's woman'. It was this last thought that she was seriously considering when something happened to her that finally confirmed the demise of the old Anna Freemont.

She stopped thinking only in terms of herself and wondered what Martin would expect her to do, even though she was not even sure that he had registered her presence in his headlong dash from the chateau. With that thought the old Anna Freemont was finally put to one side forever, and she jumped to her feet, headed for the shower and barely thirty minutes later was racing at breakneck speed in the X3 towards the slowly opening front gates. Preoccupied as she was she neglected to moderate her speed and barely cleared the still opening gates as she hurtled out onto the approach road amidst a cloud of dust and grit. She had decided to head for Auberge Fleurie and as she drove the powerful vehicle, she mulled over the news Marcel had brought earlier that day.

It concerned Monique, and was also connected to the Coubert brothers who she recalled were the Hells Angels motorbike trio she had so narrowly avoided on her initial journey to Sarony. Marcel's English was good for general conversation but he did not have an extensive vocabulary, and his ability to convey a fully rounded narrative was limited. Martin, being fluent in both French and the local patois was also able to draw on his background knowledge of the Sarony area and population to assess and decide on whatever course of action he was now engaged upon. Based on Marcel's halting explanation, Anna's understanding was that there had been some sort of fracas at Auberge Fleurie involving the Coubert brothers, during the course of which Monique had been injured.

She swung the vehicle hard left onto the Sarony road, kicked viciously and unnecessarily on the gas pedal and gasped with surprise as her head was whipped back and banged against the mercifully cushioned headrest. In the interests of public safety she eased off her speed. Despite grinding her teeth with frustration at the traffic calming measures, and low speed limit, she was soon drawing up with a squeal of tyres outside the inn.

Full of hope she slammed the car door behind her, ran around the side of the inn, and through the archway into the parking area. To her intense disappointment there was no sign of the Land Rover. She was certain that Martin would have come here and even Marcel had nodded his agreement to her suggestion that Fleurie was his likely destination. She stood, momentarily at a loss, then pulled out her mobile phone and hit the speed dial for Martin. The result was the same as when she had tried whilst getting dressed, the handset was switched off. "Fucking useless phone. Fucking stupid language." The pointless invective achieved nothing apart from allowing her a small measure of relief by venting her frustrations aloud.

Stomping into the auberge she heard the kitchen door open and Thierry sidled into the bar with the words "Bonjour M'selle." "Is Monique here Thierry?" She could not be bothered with pleasantries but forgot that Thierry's English was only marginally better than her French. He frowned and repeated "Monique?"

"Yes, er, oui. Ou est Monique?"

"Monique."

She almost hit him but fortunately an innate sense of self preservation caused him to add the word "up" and at the same time illustrate the reply with an upraised finger. Without commenting further she swept through the bar and up the narrow flight of stairs that she knew would take her to Monique's living quarters. She didn't think to knock and as soon as she entered the living room she saw it was empty. She paused in her headlong rush before guiltily edging towards the bedroom door and knocking gently. Monique's voice muffled by the woodwork drifted to her "Oui?" "C'est moi Monique, Anna." There was a noticeable pause before she heard "Entree Cherie." Turning the handle she stepped into the bedroom only to halt in the dim light before murmuring "Oh Monique."

The figure was sitting up in bed and for a moment Anna was struck dumb by the sight of the woman. Typically, it was Monique who broke the silence. "It is not as bad as it looks, the bandages make me look like a corpse."

It was not just the bandages that presented such a grotesque picture but also the bruises and swollen black eyes that restricted her field of vision to two narrow slits. In response to the injured woman's gesture Anna carefully eased herself into a sitting position on the bed, and during the course of the next hour finally learned what had occurred in Sarony on the evening before last.

As she and Martin were settling into Orville Terrace for the night the Auberge Fleurie was enjoying a quieter evening than usual. Monique had let Thierry leave early to visit his sister in the nearby village of Trouvert. Brother and sister decided to have a few drinks at the local bar and, as they sat discussing family matters, Thierry overheard the occupants of the next table mention the Coubert brothers and the name Monique Lascelles. Naturally he listened more attentively and as a result heard it said that the Coubert brothers had gone to Sarony to see if the Englishman was in the village as rumoured. They knew that he had some sort of relationship with the Lascelles woman and were going to find out from her.

Fearing trouble, Thierry phoned Auberge Fleurie and, when neither the bar phone nor Monique's number were answered, he decided to drive back to Sarony to see if everything was alright.

Meanwhile, the Coubert brothers had arrived at Auberge Fleurie and after a few drinks their rowdiness had sent the two other customers home. When Monique asked them to behave they became abusive, and when she told them to leave they turned nasty. They demanded to know whether it was true that the Englishman had turned up with a blond tart and was staying in Sarony. Monique gave them short shrift and as a result they began to slap her and push her around. The contretemps escalated as she fought back, the slaps turned to punches and it was decided to take her upstairs and teach her a real lesson. They must have been either drinking or taking drugs before they got to Sarony, for them to have lost control to such a degree at a relatively early hour in the evening, and in the ensuing struggle to drag Monique up the narrow stairs she took a severe beating until they finally reached the upstairs landing. As they relaxed momentarily, she broke free and tried to escape back down to the ground floor, but lost her footing and tumbled headlong down the entire flight.

The fall broke an arm, and badly twisted an ankle. She had also sustained a fractured cheek bone, two broken ribs, two black eyes and numerous other bruises and abrasions courtesy of the Coubert fraternity. She lost consciousness when she hit the floor of the bar, and it must have been only a matter of seconds afterwards that

Thierry came through the patio door and, being surprised to find the bar in darkness, called out and switched on the lights. Monique had gone down fighting and this sudden intrusion panicked her assailants for they had scrambled down the stairs, raced across the salon and out through the main entrance as Thierry rushed to assist the prone and bloodied woman at the foot of the stairs.

As she surveyed the battered figure Anna wondered with an inward shudder whether she would be quite so phlegmatic in Monique's place and asked "What do the police say, have they arrested the Couberts?"

Monique tried to shrug in response but the body language turned into a wince of pain.

"Surely they have caught up with them by now," persisted Anna as she passed a glass of water to the stricken figure.

No answer came as Monique held the glass to her lips, but her eyes met Anna's over the rim, and a feeling like cold electricity rippled through the blond girl's body.

"Y-you haven't called the police have you, for God's sake Monique, are you insane? But the hospital, they-they will have done won't......."

Her voice died away to nothing as Monique handed her the empty glass and resolutely kept her silence. Anna's outrage boiled over

"France is always pretending to be so sophisticated, and here you are, beaten half to death and you haven't told the police, or been to a proper hospital. You could be damaged internally Monique and, and those bastards will bloody well get away with it."

"The doctor is a good friend Cherie, he has taken care of me as you can see. There is no need for hospitals."

"If you don't tell the police, then who is going to stop them doing it again, to you or to someone else?"

The words were hardly out of her mouth before the awful truth hit home and she leapt up, ran into the bathroom, and emptied her breakfast down the toilet. When her stomach had decided to resume its normal role in life she shakily rose to her feet, rinsed out her mouth, and returned to her position on the bed. Monique raised her good arm and stroked the long blond hair as the tears began to trickle down Anna's face.

"He will be alright. I have only told you part of the story Cherie. Do not worry, things are not as bad as you think."

"Martin was here earlier wasn't he Monique?"

It was fantastic to realise that in the drama of Monique's ordeal she had completely lost sight of the reason for her race to the auberge. More frighteningly, Marcel's assertion that 'Marti will know what to do' took on an entirely new significance.

"Where is Martin, Monique?"

The question elicited a further attempt by the injured woman to calm the feelings of the uninjured woman, although the irony of that circumstance was lost on both parties.

"Marti was here Cherie, we talked and he left, but do not be afraid. Let me tell you what this is really all about and you will understand a little more what is happening. You remember I told you about how I met Marti and came to Auberge Fleurie, that I was a tart?"

Anna sniffed and nodded.

"Well, the fact is that I was a bad girl when I was growing up and mixed with bad people. Drink, drugs and a wild life that soon became no life at all. I became the worker for a man in Trouvert who was a gang boss. Not Al Capone you understand, but even so, in our small community a man to be feared. In the Summer time I would sit on my little stool by the roadside and earn my money, of which I was allowed to keep a small amount.

During one particular week things were very bad and for many reasons I earned very little. My employer concluded that I was cheating him and decided to teach me a lesson as an example to others. Although he was not a big man himself he did employ a giant named Jacek - a Pole - to ensure he was obeyed. They arrived suddenly, put me in their car and drove me along a small road that was little more than a country track. The giant held me while his boss went to work on me with his fists. They were so confident that they made no great attempt to hide, as there was nobody around.

At least that is how it appeared, but then along came Marti. He must have been watching before he showed himself because he pretended to be lost, and was smiling, jabbering away in English and waving a map just like a silly tourist. He was able to get close so that when Jacek let go of me to look at the map Marti hit him just once in the throat. They found him later that day outside the hospital, somehow both his arms were broken and he could hardly speak. It is said that he left for Poland two days later." She took another sip of her water,

"What about the other man?" Anna managed to ask, as the unbelievable narrative swirled around her head.

"Ah yes, my boss, the big shot who I was so terrified of! We drove to his house and I waited in the car as Marti dragged my powerful boss by his shirt collar into the house. Half an hour later when they returned Marti was carrying a suitcase and my boss was following, whimpering like a little dog. He couldn't carry the case himself because all of his fingers had been broken! He was crying with pain in the back of the car and I heard Marti tell him that broken fingers would mend but a broken neck could just as easily happen to a man who would hit a woman. We put him on a train South and he has never returned, his name was Andre Coubert."

Anna sat silently feeling Monique's eyes upon her as the French woman added,

"Marti gave me back my life."

"But where is he?"

"He is where he has to be, to do what he must do Cherie."

"There are three of them Monique."

"Yes, only three. Poor devils."

"What shall I do Monique?"

"You follow your heart Anna and you do the hardest thing of all which is to wait until this is over. It will be soon I promise. It was bad luck that these idiots did what they did, bad luck for them I mean. Marti may be English but he is one of us, and there is nowhere for these bastards to hide. Now either go back to the chateau or take one of my spare rooms, but I am very tired and must sleep."

Chapter 22 - Jean-Paul

Tempting as it had been to stay with Monique, Anna had driven back to the chateau, made herself a light dinner and gone to bed at around nine o'clock. The large building had taken on a mausoleum-like quality and was riddled with a variety of sounds that at night assumed orchestral proportions. Despite everything, she soon lost consciousness.

Twelve hours in the arms of Morpheus rested her but could not hold at bay the fears that crowded in when she awoke. She checked her phone to no avail and again tried Martin's number with the same result as previous attempts. The line, *'blue days, black nights'*, from the old ELO song of the seventies kept playing inside her head. She showered and dressed and, in desperate need of something to occupy her mind, began to review the notes of their trip to Italy. However hard she concentrated, her thoughts kept sliding off to dwell on what she now knew of Martin Price, and the events of several years ago when he had first met Monique.

The old Anna Freemont would have said 'I'm not doing this' and stomped off to an hotel, but the new model was a far tougher proposition. She knew that with Monique hors de combat – and she actually burst out laughing at the schoolgirl joke that it meant 'fighting tart' - it would be down to her to provide the support base he could return to. His mother was dead, Smiffy - what a bloody stupid nickname - was in Grantfield, Marcel and 'Etta were too old. So she stuck like glue to the house and its grounds for three lonely days, although that was not to say that she did nothing.

For Marcel and 'Etta it was an intriguing look at the strange English woman. Marcel, of course, was more than happy to admire the obvious physical attractions displayed by Anna as she moved around the estate. But this was merely the instinctive reaction of his biological programming; a Frenchman is a Frenchman after all. Despite being a law abiding citizen Marcel had, in common with many of his compatriots, neglected to hand in the MAC Mle 1950 automatic pistol that he had acquired during his time in the Armee de Terre. The weapon was in perfect working order and normally resided with a quantity of ammunition at the bottom of a small linen chest. Standing at his doorway or pretending to weed near his cottage, he saw her conscientiously apply a coating of dirt and grease to herself as she discovered the formula for releasing the digger from its little trailer. He watched the sly kick she gave the machine as it stubbornly refused to start and also the little leap of elation some hours later when she turned off the engine having parked the monster near the marker poles by the front gates.

So absorbed had she become in her work that Anna completely failed to appreciate that whenever she ventured outside the main house it was not long before either Marcel or 'Etta could be seen within hailing distance.

The effective firing range of a MAC Mle 1950 is approximately 50 metres!

When they were not watching over 'Marti's Woman' either Marcel or his wife took various food orders and returned laden from the Super Marché on the Dijon road. In addition, a surprising quantity of personal laundry was hung out at the rear of the chateau. All offers of practical help were politely declined although Anna did seek their advice concerning minor everyday matters on numerous occasions. One glaring oversight was corrected when Marcel took with him Anna's mobile number on an early trip into Sarony, following which Monique phoned back using her personal mobile, and private lines of communication were thus established between the two women.

The weather was warm and getting warmer, but the nights were still cool. To stay comfortable a body needed to wear a good quality sweater if venturing out once the sun had set. She walked to the main gates and back every evening using an electric torch to see her way in the dark. The old couple covertly watched from their cottage to satisfy themselves of her safe return, and occasionally glimpsed a silhouette standing in the library window before abruptly turning and fading back into the interior of the room. Each evening when they made themselves ready for bed they noted that the lights in the library remained on, and were still alight even when they finally turned their own lights out.

It was therapeutic, immersing herself in the Sarony Treasure project, but reading their notes, viewing the photos downloaded from their mobiles, and reading again the few historical references, produced nothing that could be called progress. That first evening alone Anna sat with her legs up on the settee and with a sigh tossed the last reference book onto the floor. The truth of the matter was that there was so very little reference material on the subject. She was no further forward than when they had last discussed the project a few days before, and it very much looked as if using the digger to establish the site of the chapel would be a final throw of the dice, assuming of course that Martin ever did return to the chateau. Before turning in she resolved to keep the faith through the weekend, but contact Jean-Paul if there was no word by Monday morning.

That was a course of action she was prevented from taking due to the events of the following day.

She started Friday with a plan of action that required a substantial quantity of toast, fruit juice and coffee before launching an all out assault on the library. She was determined to have every room in the living area of the chateau in pristine condition. Whilst replacing a weighty tome on one of the upper bookshelves it was necessary to stretch upwards and balance unsteadily with one leg outstretched behind her at the top of the polished wooden ladder. Just as she was poised like an oversized blond Eros her mobile phone demanded attention. The reference book crashed to the floor as she scrambled down with a lack of agility that cast severe doubts on Darwin's famous theory. Tripping over a bucket of cleaning materials she succeeded in grabbing the handset and clamping it to her ear in one clumsy movement, just before making a horizontal landing on the carpet. Half winded she heard Monique say,

"Is that you Cherie?"

"Yes, yes who else would it be?"

"Listen Cherie, the police are on their way to you?"

"The police?"

"Merde! Cherie, listen. It is Jean-Paul"

"Jean-Paul?"

"Cherie, stop repeating and listen. Mon Dieu! Jean-Paul is the policeman you met that first morning after you came to Sarony. He is coming to see you - now!"

Slowly her addled wits began to think in straight lines again.

"Martin, its Martin isn't it."

"It is about Marti yes,"

"Oh God!"

"Mon Dieu."

"Monique"

"Merde! This is no good. I will come, Thierry can drive me. Do not worry Cherie, 'allo? 'allo?"

The conversation tailed off as Anna saw from the library window the same black car that had arrived outside the auberge that morning one hundred years ago, slowly approaching along the drive, having been admitted by Marcel who was even now scurrying up the steps. She sprinted out of the library and managed to skid to a halt in time fling open the door and pre-empt Marcel by saying "It's alright Marcel, Monique just phoned me. Come in, I may need your support."

They waited together just inside the open door as the black car slowed to a halt and the tall figure of Jean-Paul emerged. He took the steps rapidly and with arm extended before him stepped into the hall. The handshake was firm, the smile friendly but, noted Anna, the tone of voice was undeniably grave as he acknowledged them both.

"Bonjour M'selle, Marcel."

"Bonjour Inspector" answered Anna in perfect Franglaise.

For a moment the three of them stood in uncertain silence until Anna realised that she was technically the hostess and stammered "W-won't you come into the libr.... oh no, er the kitchen?"

Having turned towards the library she executed a very neat change of direction and strode purposefully back along the hallway. When they were seated she addressed the policeman with a confidence she did not feel:

"How may I help you Jean-Paul?"

"When did you last see Marti?"

"Monday, Monday early afternoon."

"You are sure of that?"

"Yes."

"You did not see him perhaps yesterday, Thursday?"

"No I've just told you. I last saw him on Monday."

"Do you know where he is now - at this moment?"

"No, I've no idea. I have been very worried Jean-Paul. Please tell me what this is all about."

The policeman regarded her thoughtfully for a moment before replying.

"I will tell you now M'selle that I do not know of any reason for you to be worried, but I do need your honest replies to my questions. Now have you ever heard of a family named Coubert?"

"Yes, but not in a good sense."

"I understand you recently spoke with Monique Lascelles."

"Yes that is correct. She is a good friend."

"You know that she was beaten up by members of the Coubert family last Sunday."

"She told me what had happened when I saw her on Monday."

"When you and Marti visited her?"

"No Jean-Paul, I saw her alone. Martin had already left in the Land Rover. I followed maybe an hour later in the X3. Martin had left by the time I arrived."

"When you next see him M'selle please ask him to contact me."

"Very well Jean-Paul, but what is this all about?'

His reply caused her to drop her coffee cup with a crash onto the table.

"Early this morning the police received a phone call from a hiker who had decided to make an early beginning to his day. He claimed that what appeared to be three bodies were hanging from the Pont de Tresor"

Marcel who had struggled to follow the English conversation leapt to his feet and hurriedly mopped up the mess as Anna sat white faced with her thoughts racing. Finally she managed to whisper.

"The Coubert brothers?"

Jean-Paul nodded and sat back in his chair as he regarded the stricken English woman.

"Oh God, are they, are they dead?"

"No, unfortunately. If they were I would not be sitting here asking you to get my good friend Marti to contact me. Mind you, they are not in particularly good shape."

She slowly took in what he had said.

"You aren't going to arrest Martin?"

"Do you want me to?"

"Of course not, but I do not understand what has happened."

"When we went to Pont de Tresor we found that there were indeed three bodies hanging from it. Three naked bodies, to be precise. They were each suspended by a dozen feet of rope around their ankles from the rain channels that protrude above the ravine. The Coubert brothers had been hanging there, head down, with their hands tied behind their backs, all night. Their own underwear had been stuffed into their mouths and extremely powerful sticky tape applied to complete the gags. Ah yes the finishing touch was that their faces and genitalia had been sprayed with a bright red dye of some sort, which has so far proved completely impervious to any solvent at the disposal of the hospital."

"The hospital?"

"Yes, you see there were minor injuries such as broken noses, a few black eyes - nothing serious, but more importantly we had to check them for exposure, it was a cold night and hanging in mid air as they were! Well, once we could haul them up and free them we had to transport them, despite the smell, to the nearest hospital."

"The smell?"

"Suffice it to say M'selle that given their ordeal it was inevitable that certain bodily functions came into operation!"

She thought there was the hint of a smile in his eyes.

"But you are not going to make an arrest?"

"The Coubert brothers claim the whole incident is a prank by some of their friends, which is strange because their motorcycles have been found in the river below the bridge having apparently been thrown over the side. Thousands of Euros-worth of machines completely wrecked. Quite a prank wouldn't you say M'selle?"

"Martin is an archaeologist Jean-Paul, I am sure that he cannot be involved in this affair with the Coubert brothers, but I will of course ask him to contact you if I see him first."

"D'Accord M'selle, I must get back and take final statements from the Couberts. Au revoir."

And the tall policeman left the pair, passing as he did so a foul tempered Monique whom, with the aid of Thierry, was struggling slowly up the outside steps.

Chapter 23 - Lady Anna

The two women settled themselves in for a long wait. Marcel had trundled off shortly after Monique's arrival and, at Anna's insistence, Monique had agreed to stay until Martin's return. Thierry was more than capable of running the auberge for a few days with the help of his sister, and was happy to let the story of how he had rescued Monique from the clutches of the Couberts keep him in free drinks. Anna revelled in having company now that her worst fears had been allayed, and fussed around Monique to such an extent that the French woman said 'Cherie, I am a little damaged but not permanently crippled. Save your love for the one who needs it most."

"I don't think Martin needs me too much Monique, not with all that he has."

They were sitting together on the settee in the library and Monique sat silently before asking "Do you still not understand what this is about Cherie?"

"Of course I do, Martin was protecting you. Making sure the Couberts left you alone."

Monique's eyes although still an unhealthy colour could once again flash when she became emotional and, as Monique slowly shook her head, Anna stiffened under the intensity of the French woman's gaze.

"No Cherie. Marti was making sure that the Couberts left *you* alone. When he did not go looking for them in Trouvert they had no choice but to change their plan."

So far as Anna was concerned this latest pronouncement could as well have been delivered in Mandarin Chinese for all the enlightenment it cast.

"What plan Monique, what are you talking about?"

"To gain their revenge for the family, they intended to come after you while Marti was looking for them in Trouvert. You would have fetched a good price in Marseilles where their uncle now lives. A good revenge for what Marti did, eh?"

"Oh my God, this is fantastic. Are you telling me that all of this, this bloody nightmare, is somehow my fault?"

"Oui Cherie fantastic but true. It is not your fault, but you are the reason for it, yes. So Marti waited, and they eventually came to him, as he knew they would."

"A good soldier picks his own ground," murmured Anna.

"So he, how do you say in English? Flushed them out and dealt with them. They will never return after this humiliation Cherie, and they will dread the sound of your name. Make no mistake, Marti will have carefully explained to them the consequences of any further visit to this place."

It was at this point that they heard the front door open and close followed by firm footsteps from the hallway. A scruffy dirt streaked figure with three days growth of beard appeared in the doorway carrying a large holdall that was casually tossed to one side.

"Ah you are both here, and you are looking a lot better Monique." His eyes travelled to Anna. "And you look as wonderful as ever my love, I am so sorry that you have been put through this."

"I've suffered least of all" answered Anna "Martin, I am so relieved to see you in one piece that.................oh shit!"

The last vestige of stoic resolve evaporated and she burst into tears. Ever her guardian angel, Monique put her good arm around her shoulders and drew her tightly to her. Looking up at the begrimed figure she again assumed her imperious air and issued her orders.

"Go and clean yourself up Marti. This one cannot take any more. Come back with some cognac for all of us and then tell us what you have been doing. I have explained a little but she is confused, and I also want to hear the story. Now quickly, off you go."

It never ceased to amaze Anna how the bond between Martin and Monique was so incredibly strong. It was quite evident that each trusted the other implicitly. Whatever one told the other, it was accepted without hesitation as the pure unvarnished truth. While Monique happily dished out orders to Martin without ever considering the arrogant appearance her manner may convey to an onlooker, Martin, for his part, never thought to question or refuse to obey her. Anna also knew that Monique would have jumped to her death from the Pont de Tresor if he had so directed.

In obedience to her peremptory command Martin hurried from the room, returning forty minutes later without the several layers of filth that had accompanied him on his first appearance. He handed out the glasses and when Anna was sitting up and focussed he began to speak.

"When I heard about the attack on Monique I did exactly what the Coubert boys wanted me to do, but by the time I got to Auberge Fleurie I had cooled down. Then, when she told me how they had behaved I began to suspect a set up, so instead of continuing to Trouvert I turned back and pulled off the road, hid the Land Rover, and continued on foot. I saw you coming in the X3 at some crazy speed and barely got into the ditch before you flew past. That gave me the chance to get back into the chateau grounds without being seen, and while you were with Monique, and the Couberts were waiting to hear that I had arrived in Trouvert, I had time to figure out what was going on.

The Couberts must have sussed me when we first ran across them on the road that day I brought you to Sarony. They contacted Uncle Andre and a plan was concocted. When Monique described what had happened at the auberge it just didn't sound genuine, even the Couberts are not usually that stupid and I didn't believe they were out of control due to drugs or whatever. In which case what was the point? It could only have been to get me out of Sarony and, if so, then why?"

"To damage the chateau or take revenge on Monique?"

"No, that could be done at any time, they could have easily raided the chateau when we were in England."

"What about you? Anna asked "Why didn't you think they were after you?"

"Well they were in a manner of speaking of course, but not to physically attack me. They could have tried that any time. It was that entire drama at the auberge that gave it away because once I thought about it calmly I realised it was just a completely pointless pantomime, unless of course there was a hidden motive.

"What could that be? I don't understand."

At this point Monique interjected, "They wanted to take from Marti the thing he loves most Cherie."

For the first time Anna heard Martin reprimand his friend with a curt "Enough Monique!" before adding "I'm sorry, that was harsh – but you must let matters take their natural course."

Turning back to Anna he said "I realised that you were the target Anna. So, as I had no idea where the Couberts were I could not go after them, but had to make sure they would come to me."

"Couldn't Monique have pressed charges?"

"Yes, but she has history with the Coubert family, and that would have counted against her. She decided to wait until I got back from England so that she could see what I thought was going on, a very clever girl is our Monique. Anyway, it didn't take much to work it out so, once I had got back into the grounds, I nipped up to the chateau, pinched some supplies from the kitchen and from then on it was very easy to keep an eye on you."

"So you were here all the time!"

"That's right. When I disappeared instead of blundering into Trouvert it turned the tables on the Coubert boys. Now *they* had no idea where *I* was, and so they decided to stick with their original plan, but watch out in case I suddenly returned. They kept tabs on you, but couldn't figure out where I might be because the Land Rover was still missing. Fortunately, you stuck to the chateau. If you had decided to go joyriding I'd have had to tip you off and you wouldn't have been able to act so naturally. In the end they had to either abandon their little scheme and risk being fingered by Monique, or go for broke. They chose the wrong option last evening and the rest was easy."

"Easy? There were three of them Martin."

"Numbers aren't everything Anna. I needed to find a way to put a stop to this once and for all. I also had to make sure that when it was over you did not think I had used you as live bait, as part of an excuse to go on a killing spree. After the Calais incident I knew you thought I was some sort of psycho who enjoyed hurting people, and, as I was sure you would sooner or later find out what I did to Uncle Andre and his minder, your opinion would have been confirmed. I freely admit that when Marcel told me about them hurting Monique I thought of dumping them off the bridge without the benefit of ropes, but a public humiliation combined with putting the frighteners on them big time was a far better course of action. After what they had done to Monique I derived enormous pleasure from the expressions on their faces as I lined them up on the parapet and toppled them one by one off the bridge. It's a long way down and they saw me dump their precious bikes first."

"Was there any chance they wouldn't be found?"

"Not really, but I was prepared to let them bake in the sun throughout today before alerting Jean-Paul. As it happened they got off a bit more lightly"

There followed a lengthy silence before Anna said "Jean-Paul wants to speak to you Martin."

"Thought he might, I'll give him a call and go and see him tomorrow"

"He seems very relaxed about all this considering he's a policeman. I had a most peculiar talk with him earlier."

"Well I've known JP for some time and so he was probably just making certain you were OK."

"Oh, he seemed quite keen to contact you."

"He will only want to be sure the matter is over for good. This is his patch after all."

"And is it?"

"Yes, even Uncle Andre is fairly small time despite his apparently big Marseilles connections and the Coubert lads are now in no doubt just what will be coming after them if they step out of line again."

"I'm not sure I understand Martin."

"But *they* do Anna."

The momentous day petered out with Monique insisting on returning to the auberge now that Anna was no longer alone, and Martin visiting the Moranes and then phoning Jean-Paul. They went to bed early and by the time Anna had undressed Martin had fallen into a deep sleep, sprawled like a starfish on the big bed. So she took herself off to what she now thought of as her own room.

By the time he staggered back into the land of the living many hours later Anna had been up for a couple of hours and breakfast was quickly available.

"Sorry about last night," he smiled "I just closed my eyes for a moment and bang, it was morning. Are you fit for a session with the digger or have you had enough and want to go home?"

"I'm happy to carry on for as long as it makes sense, and I will be happy to demonstrate my prowess with that monstrous machine. My time alone wasn't entirely wasted you know."

She half expected him to take the bait and jump to Mickey's defence but instead he looked intently at her and said "I can't tell you how much it meant to me when I saw you staying on at the chateau and not running for England."

"I thought about it Martin, and for a short while I felt as if everything was crashing down around me. This may sound stupid but I was always the tallest one in the class when I was at school and so for some reason I was expected to act a lot older than the others in my age group. Then when I grew boobs it got even worse, because at the age of fourteen I had the body of an eighteen year old. All I ever wanted was to be nice and anonymous and just be me. So I started to keep myself to myself and avoid any situation where I was the one carrying other people's expectations. When you took off the other day I was very tempted to pull out because I didn't know what was happening or what I should do. I finally realised that if I did run then I would be leaving behind everything I had gained since I came to Sarony, and to borrow heavily from your soldier's lexicon 'what we have, we hold'."

He leaned forward and took her hand "I think that when we finish this project we should throw a party here at the chateau, and invite our friends from England as well. A chateau really does need a grand lady as hostess, and ever since I first saw you in full sail down Grantfield High Street I've imagined you standing at the top of the steps at the front of the house welcoming guests."

She felt herself blushing and said "We seem to have come a long way very quickly don't we."

The mood changed subtly and he replied "And before we get carried away I suppose we had better see if that chapel ever did have a vault. Come on Lady Anna lets get Mickey to earn his keep."

'Etta stood gazing out of her kitchen window and watched as the couple walked along the drive towards the distant front gates. There was something fluid about the way they walked together, almost as if their movements were synchronised by some invisible choreographer. She had no doubt that Marti had found his woman and hoped, with all her heart, that the woman had found her man.

Chapter 24 - Proposal

It took an hour of careful work to establish that they had not put the first trench as close to the supposed rear wall as hoped. A second trench was dug from the centre point of the first and at a right angle travelling away from where they thought the rear wall of the chapel had been. This time they struck what they were looking for, the second trench neatly bisected an old wall at a depth of about twelve inches. They then followed the line of that wall, first in one direction, and then the other, until they were satisfied that they had managed to expose the foundation of the entire length of rear wall.

"Well our original effort wasn't too far off the mark was it," commented Martin. "Any thoughts on where an entrance to the vault could be, assuming there was one of course?"

"I've been trying to picture in my mind the layout of a rear entrance to an underground vault, and it seems to me that if we make the assumption that a vault existed, then it is reasonable to assume it was purpose built, and probably not just a converted cellar that someone thought 'oh that's a good place to stick grandpa's body'."

"Go on."

"In that case it would have been designed with a practical eye and so the fact that a coffin or something of the sort needed to be taken into the vault, not to say a body or two, means that it would be sensible to have steps that were not too steep. If the steps are directly opposite the entrance then that means there would be less manoeuvring necessary once at the bottom, but on the other hand you would need to dig out quite a large area to accommodate the length of the steps and also at least one and a half times the length of a coffin once it had reached the bottom."

"I'm impressed, you really have thought deeply about this haven't you."

"Well, a girl's got to occupy her time when the lord of the manor has pushed off for a few days summer camp, but I haven't finished yet. I think that our builders will have opted for a flight of steps dropping down from one of the sides in parallel with the rear wall and probably right up against it. When a coffin reached the bottom it would still need to be turned ninety degrees, but even so, the sunken access area would be a lot smaller than if the steps were set opposite the vault entrance. So my money is on the side access steps, and quite frankly I think that the entrance would be in the centre of the chapel rear wall regardless of where the steps may be, particularly if we are dealing with what is known as a barrel vault. That would mean that the highest part of the vault was the centre."

"So you reckon we should dig down from a centre point flush against that rear wall?"

"Exactly! We don't need to bother looking for steps, but even so it will mean quite a lot of digging as presumably we will want to actually get down to the floor level of the access area. I reckon we could end up digging down as much as ten feet before we get there."

"OK Anna, I'm happy to go with your idea. As we are not anticipating finding archaeology of any known value I'll use Mickey to do all of the hard work, and perhaps you would rummage through what I dig out just in case there is anything of interest."

"Alright, do you think we can quickly ascertain whether a vault actually exists?"

"Yes, if there is no vault then I reckon we will hit the bottom of the foundation at around four feet, and if we expose a wall continuing below that depth then we should be onto a winner. Mind you, I'm not exactly sure what we will find."

"It's difficult to make any sort of guess isn't it. In fact the whole vault idea is in itself complete speculation, let alone what it may or may not contain. Even if we do strike lucky we don't know whether it will be any use at all as far as our project is concerned."

"Right, well let's get at it. If you would like to note the centre of the wall and then measure three feet either side and mark out a couple of guide lines with those marker poles then a spread of six feet should be enough to let us locate the access point if there is a vault."

She watched as he expertly positioned the digger and scooped out the first load of earth before backing up, moving a few feet to one side, and dumping the soil. The pile of excavated material slowly grew as the long articulated arm of the digger frequently returned to take bites with its hungry mechanical mouth. Anna used a long garden rake to probe and break up the earth and turn over quantities of rubble on the off-chance that something worthwhile could come to light. Hardly scientific she thought, but this was really nothing more than a homeowner indulging in a bit of landscaping, and she found no hint that anything of genuine interest was likely to be buried in the outside earth.

Progress was swift and as a vertical shaft six feet deep and two yards wide was dug out it soon became clear that the lower masonry being uncovered was substantially more extensive than mere foundations. Martin continued to work the digger downwards until with an audible thump the arm jolted against something more unyielding than the compacted earth and debris encountered thus far. The muddied elongated area of wall that was now uncovered disclosed little as he had taken pains not to scrape the excavator blades against the vertical surface for fear of damaging something vital. Anna sat alongside the hole and peered at the exposed segment of wall. She felt tired from the energetic raking she had been doing through the accumulating soil and was quite content to fall in with Martin's suggestion that they call a halt for the day, clean themselves up and eat dinner on the terrace.

Sitting there that warm evening Anna could not resist raising the matter of the Couberts by asking "Would you really have killed them?"

He looked at her for a long time before responding.

"I'm not sure that's a fair question, but I will say that in certain circumstances then yes, I would. But let me now ask you whether you trust me?"

She was momentarily taken aback before answering "Yes, of course I do."

"There's no 'of course' about it, you mistrusted me a few weeks ago to such an extent that you jumped ship, and it's only by a fluke that you didn't end up back in Grantfield. Since then I think you've changed your view of me, haven't you?."

"Yes I have, my initial judgement was wrong, and to be quite frank I wouldn't sleep with you if I didn't trust you."

"In that case your original question becomes irrelevant doesn't it?"

"I don't see why."

"The reason is that, if knowing what you now know about me you trust me enough to sleep with me, then surely you must also trust me to make an honest decision rather than one based solely on a need to satisfy some innate blood lust? What I did when I first met Monique was maybe appalling to your sensibilities, but the fact is that Uncle Andre and his Polish heavy were exceptionally bad guys, and I stopped them dead in their tracks and cleared them out of the region. This time round I dealt with the Coubert riff-raff in a different manner and I guarantee you they will not be back."

"Is that another way of saying that the end justifies the means?"

"Absolutely not, I'm saying that appropriate measures are necessary to achieve a defined objective, and I have to be trusted to make an honest decision."

She nodded slowly and replied "I no longer mistrust your motives, it's just that the level of violence you are capable of, albeit on a disciplined basis, takes some getting used to. It's much harder than if you were some loony who occasionally got drunk and into a fight in a pub for instance. Just the fact that you have the ability to employ a lethal level of violence is quite unnerving. The ordinary man in the street doesn't have that, or rather although theoretically capable, hasn't been trained to develop it."

He nodded "Fair enough, but it's not impossible for you to live with that fact is it?"

"No, not now that I understand the man, and the fact that he only chooses to resort to this dubious skill on mercifully rare occasions. I don't like it Martin, but its part of the man sitting in front of me."

They subsided into silence for a few moments, not making eye contact as they pursued their private thoughts.

"Martin, have we just had our first row?"

"Possibly, if so it was fairly painless wasn't it?"

"Yes, completely."

"Good, because it would be unfortunate if you had to spend the rest of your life with a man who caused you pain."

It was seven o'clock in the evening and the voice of the wren filled the suddenly empty air. The clink that Martin's glass made as he replaced it on the table sounded like an entire shelf full of china crashing to the floor. Anna launched into her world famous impression of a pet goldfish behind the glass of its bowl as she failed to synchronise vocal chords with lip movement, and in sympathy the wren fell silent. When her faculties finally returned she heard a voice that sounded almost like her own, say,

"If that was a proposal the answer is yes."

He stood up and walked towards the kitchen saying "In that case I'll get us some champagne."

Chapter 25 - Francois

The following day saw them make an early start and by mid-morning the excavation measured six feet by ten, with a depth of twelve. With water ferried carefully in an old water butt, they energetically scrubbed the exposed wall. Once the sticky sub-soil had been washed from its surface they could see that from their lower ground level up to a height of eight feet the stone wall blocks were of slightly different dimensions and colour to those rows running above them.

"It looks as if we've struck oil and your thoughts about the vault entrance are spot on," stated Martin as they surveyed their handiwork. "Now we've cleaned things up it's obvious that there was an opening of some sort that has been filled in by a different hand to that of the original builder."

She ran her palm over the dressed stone blocks and said "It's nice to be proved right about something to do with Chretien. This is the first truly original discovery we have made, although without your stepfather's clue about the wife and son we probably wouldn't even have thought about looking for a family vault."

"And we will need to take a run into Dijon and find a plant hire shop. It looks to me as if we will need to rent a couple of Acrows, a nice sledge hammer, a portable generator, and one or two other bits and pieces. Come on, let's get cracking, the sooner we get the stuff, the sooner we get into the vault."

Once again the Land Rover proved its worth, but the visit to Dijon left Anna wondering how it was that the men who worked in such places could be so similar whether based in Dijon or Dagenham. She was certain that the entire transaction was carried out without the Frenchman once making any sort of visual contact with Martin, as he had his eyes firmly riveted to her bust from the moment they entered the trade counter area. Martin also noticed and commented as he loaded the Land Rover, "I'll have to take you with me on these shopping trips more often. That guy was so interested in your equipment he didn't charge me for all of his."

"Well I'm so thrilled to have made a worthwhile contribution in the masculine world of plant hire" she snorted. "Let's get going. I feel as if I've had grubby hands on me."

It took the rest of the day to widen by a foot or two the exposed area of vault wall and apart from a few fragments of roof tiles, some musket balls, and two low value coins, the freshly enlarged pit yielded nothing apart from more pieces of rubble that must have come from the chapel itself. The finale and also the anticlimax of the day's work occurred when Martin took his sledgehammer to the wall. Having removed two stone blocks he decided that they would let the vault air freshen up over night while they enjoyed a leisurely supper before returning to the task the following morning.

The next day's work started slowly as sufficient blocks were first loosened, and then removed until a narrow vertical opening was created. To Anna's frustration

Martin then insisted on inserting a metal RSJ overhead and supporting it with the Acrows, before pronouncing the entrance safe, and inviting her to be the first person to step into the cool dark cavern for several hundred years.

Daylight did not spread far into the vault and the first impression was of a murky, gloomy interior with a central aisle and patches of vague grey outlines on either side. The forward view soon faded into blackness as the chamber depth proved too great for the light to fully penetrate. Despite having some fresh air introduced, there was still a noticeable dry, earthy, odour that added a heaviness to the atmosphere. A cursory glance as they played their torches around the underground chamber revealed quite a number of stone coffins but Martin almost immediately retreated back into the morning sunlight with the words "It won't take long to rig up the temporary lighting, I'll move the generator closer and we'll have the place lit up like Blackpool in no time."

Half an hour later they re-entered the vault, and with a reasonable light level powered by the small generator happily chugging away outside, they were able to obtain a clearer view of their subterranean surroundings. It was obvious that the chamber was constructed in the shape of a long oval – half barrel shape - with the length matching, as far as they could judge, the probable length of the original chapel structure that was once above ground. The vault roof, although giving plenty of clearance directly above the central aisle, curved gently down to ground level on either side, with the aisle itself being some six feet wide and extending in a dead straight line into the gloom at the far end of the chamber. Each side was divided into narrow bays containing raised stone platforms on which coffins could be placed. The builders had anticipated generations of the Sarony line finding their final resting places in this family tomb, but it was clear from the many unoccupied plinths that this expectation had not been fulfilled.

"There are probably no more than thirty or forty coffins down here" said Anna in a disappointed tone as they looked around the musty underground chamber. "Although there seems to be plenty of room it looks as if only a few of these side niches are actually occupied."

"That bears out your idea that the vault dropped out of use quite early on. Let's see exactly how far this place extends." replied her companion as he strolled down towards the far end of the vault.

Anna was about to ask whether he wanted to make an immediate start on mapping out the vault and trying to identify its occupants when his voice echoed back to her.

"Hey Anna, come and take a look at this."

She hurried the length of the vault and saw that he was standing alongside a small niche at the very end in which a stone coffin rested without its cover. The cover was standing on end against the far side of the plinth. It had first caught Martin's eye due to its size which was only half that of the others, but now, as Anna joined him, he leaned forward and peered at the exposed dusty skeletal remains.

"Good state of preservation considering its age" he murmured.

She nodded as she also stared at what had once been a young person. "Look Martin, something awful happened to the child, the entire lower rib cage and vertebrae are broken and crushed."

"It looks to me as if we've at last solved the mystery of the missing son and heir" he grunted.

"Do you think so?"

"Looks about the right age and it's the only small coffin that I could see, although there may be other children's remains further back in the rows on either side."

"So what could have killed him, it looks as if something heavy fell on him."

"Yes, although something like a block of stone or a tree trunk would have crushed a far greater area. Rather than an impact injury it's as if intense pressure was slowly applied to a very narrow area."

"You don't think he was tortured to death do you?"

"I suppose anything is possible, but no, I don't think that's the answer. This isn't the only item of interest at this end of the vault though, and that's another thing. All of the other bodies are at the opposite end near the entrance, but there are just two down here at the far end. Look at this adult one Anna. Something very interesting caught my eye as I came past. Let me show you."

She followed him a few paces back and in the last occupied niche on the other side he stopped. She joined him and, leaning over to look at the cover, she was able to make out the name of the occupant. Martin however drew her back by the arm to the aisle and pointed to a crudely carved inscription facing them on the end of the stone coffin where the feet of the deceased would have rested. Anna peered at the script as Martin asked,

"How's your Latin?"

"It's her isn't it, it's his wife in the portrait – Mathilde Eugenie, that's what is carved on the cover, and oh my goodness is this other wording saying what I think it is?"

"I'm afraid so. *Suicidium* certainly means suicide, and if I'm not mistaken this other group of words is *'excommunicatus lata sententia'*. This inscription on the end panel states that she has been booted out of the Roman Catholic church because she killed herself."

Anna mulled over his statement before asking, "Wouldn't the chapel and this vault have been a consecrated site?"

"Yes, without doubt."

"Then how is it that she is interred down here - suicides couldn't be accepted on consecrated ground in those days."

He smiled suddenly and said "Let's take a walk in the sun shall we, it seems to me that we've unravelled the last two mysteries from Armand's notes. I think I can hazard a reasonable guess at what may have happened."

Anna wasn't sorry to leave the gloom of the vault, and the warmth of the sun felt good as they emerged into daylight. They climbed out of the trench and walked slowly across the grass towards the chateau as Martin launched into his explanation.

"Let's suppose young Francois was killed in some unfortunate mishap and that once he is laid to rest his stricken mother returns to the vault to look at her poor son's body, maybe she even makes a number of visits. If the portrait is anything to go by, they only had the one child and so, as with the death of any child, it would have hit her very hard. Supposing though, she is completely traumatised, perhaps feels responsible in some way for the boy's death? With the chapel being so close to the chateau itself maybe she does make repeated visits to the boy's coffin, and finally even goes so far as to remove the cover. That would explain why the lad's body was exposed, and maybe the grieving mother goes completely over the edge and kills herself. In fact, maybe she commits suicide on one of her visits."

She remained silent for a moment before saying, "It's a compelling theory Martin I admit, but how could she be interred on consecrated ground?"

"I honestly don't believe a professional soldier such as Chretien will have laid much store by the rites of the church. That's not to say he didn't believe in God, I'm sure he did, but we are talking here about a man who has earned a living from his skill in bloody hand to hand combat, and I can tell you that experience puts a lot of things into perspective."

She again remained silent as they walked slowly over the grass. This was as close as he had come to revealing even a small glimpse of his army service, and even then it was only to somehow show support for a long dead fellow professional.

After a moment Martin continued. "Regardless of the view of the church Chretien decides to inter her in the vault but, not surprisingly, runs into opposition from the local clergy who, when he persists, go so far as to add that inscription to the coffin."

"Alright, it's a good hypothesis although we've got nothing to support it have we?"

"Well let's add a bit more colour to the scene then. We know a little of Chretien's character and it seems certain to me that he wouldn't put up with being pushed around by a bunch of local witch doctors. I reckon he puts his wife's body into the vault regardless. The clergy retaliate by declaring the chapel to be in a state of desecration, and so the vault and maybe the chapel as well are doubly desecrated, first by the suicide and then by Chretien insisting on her ladyship remaining there.

Let's face it, however fondly we may choose to regard Chretien, he was a man not to be messed with. On his home territory in his role as local lord of the manor he didn't have to put up with any nonsense from the mumbo-jumbo merchants concerning where his poor wife could be laid to rest. My betting is that he told them to go to hell and sent them scuttling back to their bishop. Even so, with God on their side maybe they actually go so far as to have Chretien himself declared excommunicate. He refuses to back down, boots the clergy off his land – or maybe worse - and seals up the vault entrance. Shortly afterwards he ships out with Henry Tudor, and perhaps never returns to France. In fact, the scandal over the wife could be the reason he joined up with Henry as part of what was a rather speculative and highly dangerous adventure."

"Well Sherlock, I'm impressed and must say that all sounds very plausible, but I've got one big question for the great detective."

"Ask away Watson."

"How does this help us so far as the Sarony Treasure is concerned?"

"No idea whatsoever," came the demoralising reply.

By this time they had walked in a large circle and were sitting on the edge of the trailer enjoying the warming sun.

"Your theory would certainly account for the facts as we know them," said Anna rubbing his upper arm with her hand.

He smiled at her and she stopped rubbing but didn't remove her hand.

"Look at me," she said "Can't keep my hands off you"

"I'm not complaining" he grinned "Just knowing you want to touch me makes my head spin. I wonder if that is how Chretien felt about his wife and son? Am I just transferring elements of my own personality to a man who died over five hundred years ago? It's all very well my theory hanging together, but that's all it is, just a theory."

"I don't think it's a matter of transference, I reckon you are similar characters and maybe that's why you seem to fit in so well here in Sarony. Let's get back to the vault Martin, we can take a more thorough look round and then decide what to do next. Will you have to report the discovery to the French authorities?"

"Probably, although there is no great rush. I expect they will simply send someone down to take a look, and log it all in their records. There's nothing unusual or valuable to get the archaeological world excited, nor the government for that matter.

I think I may have a proper entrance built and uncover the whole of the original access area, perhaps have a word at the local church and see if some sort of ceremony can be arranged to make it a better place again. Surely there must have been some progress made in these matters over the last five hundred years? Oh, now what have I said to get the old spinster lady fired up?"

She had turned as they walked and pressed herself firmly against him causing him to stumble to a halt. "I'm still amazed by the fact that you have such a gentle side to your character."

"Well I couldn't sleep easy at night if I didn't make some attempt to put things right, it's not much to ask to be laid to rest for eternity in peace and free from some nasty aspersion conjured up by fools is it? How would you feel now that we've found them if every morning when you woke up they were still lying there deprived of what was important to them? It's all part of the responsibility of owning this estate, a duty of care that I feel more and more the longer I spend here."

She smiled and pressed against him even more firmly "It's a good thing we are out here in the open Martin Price, because the more I know of you the more I like, and the more I want."

"Well contain yourself Miss Freemont because not only has 'Etta the eyes of a hawk, she would take a very dim view of any saucy goings on in plain view. Didn't your dad ever tell you how nice girls should behave in public?"

"My dad, I'll have you know, thinks I can do no wrong and, would you believe, in private still refers to me as his little treasure. He used to say it all the time until I explained that it was a bit embarrassing in front of boyfriends and not entirely appropriate given my height."

He laughed and squeezed her arm. "I suppose it must be difficult for a man to realise that his little girl has become the object of lust and debauchery in other men's eyes"

"Well let's get today's work finished first shall we Mr Price. Then if we have got the time and energy… well, who knows what could happen!"

The initial elation at the discovery of the vault and the investigation of its contents had left them feeling a little deflated due to the fact that they now seemed to be at another dead end so far as their search was concerned. They made a second more methodical examination of the burial chamber but elicited from it no new discoveries and, it was as they were about to step back out into the late afternoon sun, that Anna stopped and grabbed Martin by the arm saying "Hang on a minute, can we go back to the boy's coffin and put the cover back in place. I know it's been leaning against the side almost since the day he was put down here but, as you said earlier, we do have a responsibility to show him a little bit of respect don't we."

They walked back down to the far end of the aisle and between them were easily able to lift the coffin lid up and slide it into place, giving some privacy to the pathetic remains that had lain exposed for so many years. Unlike the other adult coffins which carried carved images of the occupants on their surfaces, the small boy's casket was simply engraved with his name and some Latin script. As they brushed the centuries accumulation of dust and grit from it Anna noticed some additional words etched carefully along the lowest part of the surface.

"Look Martin, it seems we can't get away from the word today."

" *'Notre Trésor'* means Our Treasure. It seems Francois had doting parents just like your father.

They tidied up the site, hung stout tarpaulin across the entrance and drove the Land Rover slowly back to the main house. Martin took the time to speak with the Moranes and give them the news about the vault before trudging back and heading for a warm bath.

Chapter 26 - Chretien

For the first time since their arrival in France they awoke
to the sound of rain, and watched from the comfort of the
large double bed as the water ran down the long multi-
paned bedroom windows.

"I've been thinking" said Martin as he propped himself
up on one elbow.

"Should I feel alarmed?" She giggled.

"Not about that. I've been thinking about Chretien and
his treasure, and something has just dropped into place
that I should have picked up on yesterday"

"Have we missed something?"

"Not exactly, it's more that we have not put something
into the correct context. You remember yesterday when
you told me your dad used to refer to you as his little
treasure?"

"Yes of course."

"Well it was only an hour or so afterwards that we
replaced the lid of Francois' coffin and discovered that
his parents had etched the words 'Our Treasure' on it in
addition to the usual religious prayers. Now supposing
they were like your dad, and instead of being just a
farewell comment on the lines of, for instance, 'the light
of our lives', the word 'treasure' was a normal everyday

endearment that they used for Francois; just like your dad uses it for you?"

"Perhaps it was, but how does that affect our research?"

"It wouldn't have any significance were it not for that bit of parchment that McEwan brought to our attention when we were at Poligny, and that Smiffy later confirmed as genuine. Can we hop down to the library and have a look at the copy Smiffy scanned over to us?"

"Oh all right if you are sure you want do it right now, I can see that living with you is going to be one long party. Pass me that spare dressing gown and let's get going."

They stood looking at the screen and Martin read again aloud:

'I Chretien de Sarony confess that having lost forever the treasure that occupied every waking and sleeping moment of my thoughts on my weary journey from Frosinore I now lay to rest my beloved wife Mathilde Hermione who has filled my years in England with what joy I now have found in the service of the English King. I have never truly recovered from having the greatest wealth imaginable snatched from me within sight of the safety of my home and hope my feeble efforts have dear wife given you some small recompense for your devotion to one incapable of providing the love you had the right to expect.'

"Now we have read this as referring to the treasure he took from Italy, but the entire message is really an apology from a grieving man to a woman for never really meeting up to what he thinks were her rightful expectations. He lays the blame on the loss of his treasure that 'occupied every waking and sleeping moment', and then goes on to rue the loss of the 'greatest wealth imaginable'. OK, the loss of the treasure would have been pretty galling at the time, but it wasn't as if he was impoverished. He was wealthy landed gentry, and it had all happened some ten years earlier. In between times he had formed part of the Tudor suicide mission to take the crown and come up trumps. So why would he bring the matter of the treasure up at such a sensitive moment if it merely referred to gold and valuable items? More to the point, it's all completely over the top if describing the Italian loot, don't you think?"

"You think he is referring to Francois?"

"Since our findings yesterday, yes I do. It's an interpretation that makes sense of several things. It ties in very nicely with the words on the coffin. It makes more sense as the object of the comments in the parchment, and more to the point it explains why it is so baffling that the gold should have been stolen in an ambush at the most inappropriate point on the route home."

"He says it was taken from him within sight of home doesn't he."

Martin leaned back against desk and folded his arms. "Back in the fifteenth century the bridge down the road was made of wood and I suspect it was not always kept in a state of good repair. Now what if Mathilde Eugenie had travelled to Colmierre to meet the returning hero, and

Francois accompanied her. On the way back the boy manages to end up under the wheels of Chretien's wagon. That would account for the injury we saw yesterday, imagine a wheel moving slowly across that small body. It's lucky it didn't cut him clean in half."

"Very impressive Mr Price, but why should the accident have occurred on the bridge?"

"It's always been assumed that the name of the bridge originated from Chretien returning home with his loot but surely if an accident occurred on the bridge that killed the boy, then perhaps Chretien himself gave it that name or, more likely 'Treasure's Bridge'. Across the decades it was assumed that the name referred to the Italian gold when in fact it referred to Francois. There never was an ambush, just a dreadful accident."

"It certainly does make sense, but there is no way of proving it is there?"

"Not that I can see, but it does pose further questions regarding the loot, because if it wasn't stolen from Chretien then he must have brought it here to Sarony, but if so what the hell did he do with it?"

"I don't think he ever brought it to Sarony."

"What makes you say that?"

"First of all the fact that a ton weight of gold seems to have just vanished without trace, but secondly something you happened to say a minute ago. You said the boy was lucky not to have been cut in half but it's quite clear that if he had been slowly rolled over by a weight of more than a ton he would have been. Or at least the crushed bones would have been more like powder than what we saw."

"Meaning that the wagon was not so heavily laden as we would suppose?"

"Yes."

"So, young Anna, as we have moved our research into the world of un-provable theories where do you think Chretien stashed the lolly?"

"It can only have been somewhere along his route home, but there is something I've had nagging away in the back of my mind that is connected with the return journey and I can't pin it down."

"You mean Chretien's return journey, not ours I imagine."

"Yes, Chretien's, it was something either in the notes or our discussions. I remember at the time thinking it was odd, but it wasn't odd enough to make me give it any great attention. It was just something that pinged in my head and I thought 'oh, I thought such and such' and then I forgot all about it. To give you a plain answer I can only guess that he stashed the treasure somewhere along the route, but that goes without saying doesn't it."

"So let's do a final review of our raw information starting with Armand's notes and see if we can pick up the threads. Heaven knows we have so little that it won't take us very long, and what about going over to see Monique on Saturday and eating and drinking far too much?"

"That sounds good, we can at least see how she is looking now, and you've spoken to her on the mobile haven't you?"

"That's right, she said she is feeling ok now although her arm is restricting her more than she likes. But she's a tough bird is Monique and she will come through this none the worse for the experience."

Several hours passed as they examined all of the material concerning their search for the elusive treasure, and for Anna it was the third time she had ploughed through the references and photographs. Towards the end they took a break for refreshment and Martin phoned Monique to arrange a table for Saturday. Although Anna could not follow his French, the conversation caught her attention when, having said something, she heard the buzz of Monique's voice respond and cause him to roar with laughter and finish the call.

"What was the joke?"

"Oh, Monique told me that they are planning rabbit for Saturday and would that be OK? I said that surely a visit from the lord of the manor and his lady warranted a little more than some road kill."

"How rude, what did she say?"

"She made some extremely colourful biological references to me followed by the suggestion that if the lord of the manor would like to find an ox, then she would happily prepare a traditional meal for him. What's the matter Anna why are you looking like that, it's only friendly banter."

"Ox, yes that's the thing we've been looking for. The thing I couldn't pin down. Chretien used oxen to pull his wagon didn't he."

"Yes I think so, but so what?"

"When I was doing my degree I had to make a short study of farming methods in medieval times and I learned that oxen where widely used because they were cheaper to feed and maintain than horses, and also had far greater staying power. They would trudge steadily along for hour after hour although they were of course much slower. Now correct me if I'm wrong, but Chretien actually employed a team of two didn't he?"

"I believe so, that is according to one of his travelling companions. He bought a cart and team from a farmer at Frosinone."

"That's what I thought, now I also recall that ox teams are a little peculiar in that the two creatures form a sort of bond which often develops to such an extent that they don't like being physically separated."

"A bit like us?"

"Oh ha-ha. Now behave and listen. It can be a bit of a problem to replace one of them if an animal dies, and it looks as if this is what happened to Chretien's team. Now the less talkative companion mentions that the oxen 'were still not fully at ease and the road from Vigevano… etc' which indicates to me that the new ox was put in place at Vigevano."

"So what is odd about that?"

"When you were off on your Coubert hunt I went back through all of our material. I noticed that amongst the photographs we took at the little museum in Campomorto were receipts for purchases made by Chretien, one of which was for the purchase of a single ox. That ox must be a replacement because they had already bought a team of two from a farmer and, as mentioned, this creature was still not fully at ease by the time they got back on the road."

"I must be exceptionally dim Anna, but I cannot for the life of me see what bearing this has on our problem concerning the treasure."

"It's the date of the receipt for the single ox." She was tapping at the computer as she spoke and added "Look, here is the photo you took at the museum. It's dated a month later than the battle at Frosinone."

"And?"

"Oh Martin, if he only bought the replacement a whole month after the battle - and the companion says the oxen were still not fully at ease, then what was he doing that took a month to get from Frosinone to Vigevano? It's only twenty-five miles. More to the point, if you say it would take 125 days *fully laden* to get all the way to

Sarony, then how come, according to the dates of departure and arrival, it actually did take that long? This would mean that despite them having spent a month apparently hanging around within 25 miles of Frosinone he then covered most of the distance - Vigevano to Sarony - in only 100 days?"

"Brilliant. He could only have made it if he was carrying a far lighter load than a ton of gold."

"Yes. That's what was bugging me, I thought something sounded off key but couldn't nail it down."

"So he no doubt had a few items aboard and almost certainly there was enough money to pay off his companions to their satisfaction, and we know they had at least one mule as well as their horses."

"And that must mean either he couldn't be bothered to buy the replacement ox earlier while he was kicking his heels at Vigevano or, one of the ox team died suddenly just as he was due to leave. In order to keep to his schedule he had to get the show on the road despite knowing the possible difficulties in the animals getting used to each other. He knew he could still cover the remaining distance in the required time because of the light load even though the animals weren't fully settled."

"Hold on Anna. You have just used the words 'schedule' and 'the required time' as if he was working to some form of pre-arranged plan."

"I think he was in a manner of speaking. He knew darned well how long it should take him to get to Sarony with a ton of gold, and so would plenty of other people, and so he bided his time somewhere between Frosinone and Vigevano for a month."

"Oh I see, very clever. If attacked on the road after Vigevano he could if necessary bolt for it on horseback because the loot wasn't on the wagon, and if he wasn't attacked then everybody thinks he's got it safely back to the family chateau. Either way he can beetle off to wherever he's hidden it at some later date when the heat is off. Anna you are a genius."

"Also, and I admit that I've only just thought of this, he's clever enough to make the occasional donation in gold for shrines etc while he is travelling, to reinforce the idea that he's got the loot with him. You know what Martin? If I didn't have the hots for you I think I could fall for our Chretien, what a clever chap."

"But it all came unravelled within sight of home didn't it. He lost his son, his wife almost certainly topped herself, and he suddenly realised that the only things really worth a light had been taken from him. So he broods for a while, finds himself another woman, and joins a suicide mission to claim the crown of England."

"So where does that leave us?"

"A very good question. I think you've almost single-handedly solved the mystery of Chretien's treasure Anna. Somewhere between Frosinone and Vigevano is where we must look, and that's a distance of say 25 miles."

Chapter 27 - Dinner

A warm evening enjoying good food on a terrace in a French village takes a lot of beating, and when the company is good it becomes the very best way to spend leisure time. When Anna looked back to how she floated through those hours on a mix of adrenalin, alcohol, and relief, it always felt like one of the very best evenings of her life. She entered the auberge with Martin's arm firmly around her waist and this time there was no sarcastic nasal voice to break the spell. Monique met them as they emerged onto the patio and the warmth of her greeting reassured Anna that their appearance as most definitely 'a couple' caused nothing but pleasure.

In deference to Anna the conversation was conducted entirely in English with no secret asides or private jokes. They were joined unexpectedly, as the meal itself finished, by Jean-Paul who laughingly explained how the Coubert brothers had resorted to wearing women's makeup to cover the red facial dye.

"Tell me Marti, how long before the redness fades?"

"About two years given exposure to the air."

"And the other parts?"

"Longer - perhaps three."

"You are a hard man Marti, but I knew that when we served together."

Anna pricked up her ears. "I didn't know the two of you were in the......."But she knew she was too late from the look that flashed silently between the two men.

"I was simply a liaison officer with Marti's regiment for a short time" replied the policeman unconvincingly, and the moment had passed.

Both Jean-Paul and Monique listened attentively as Martin related the story of the siege of Frosinone and their conjectural reconstruction of the events behind the well known local legend of the Sarony Treasure. Murmurs of appreciation greeted the explanation that the two archaeologists had pieced together. They both asked if they could see the vault and its contents and when Martin said he intended throwing a summer party, he added that the vault would be made accessible to everyone.

"I think early September will be a likely time. That will give us time to organise the work that needs to be done on the vault and one or two other things, including trying to get into the mind of a fifteenth century French knight."

"It has been obvious to me for some time that you two are let us say, closer, than when I first met Anna here a few weeks ago," remarked Jean-Paul, "And it is clear from your presence together this evening that you are now very close indeed. I hope I do not embarrass you by asking if the 'other things' you referred to a moment ago have a bearing on your feelings for each other?"

They both looked at the elegant policeman then at each other before Anna nodded, and Martin replied,

"I am impressed that the police force trains it's people so well that they have such super sensitive deductive powers JP."

The policeman laughed and said "Mon ami, I have rarely seen two people so enamoured of each other. The police force cannot take credit for the fact that I am a Frenchman and therefore I know these things."

"Well said Jean-Paul, we French invented love did we not?" This was Monique's contribution.

"OK, OK, you two," laughed Martin. "We have decided to not only move things onto a permanent footing but also to go the whole hog and get hitched, so yes that is one of the other things."

"And maybe by then we will have discovered the location of the treasure," added Anna, "although a 25 mile stretch is a lot of territory when the trail is over five hundred years old."

"Huh, you English have no imagination" pouted Monique. "I know where I would have put it if I had been Le Comte de Sarony."

Silence descended and three pairs of eyes swivelled in her direction as she helped herself to another glass of wine.

"You mean you know that part of Italy?" It was Anna who asked.

There came a further infuriating pause as Monique took a sip from her glass before replying,

"I have never been there Cherie. Why should I need to have been to Italy?" Came the surprising reply.

"So you think he got it into France?" Asked a baffled Anna.

Another pause as Monique enjoyed her wine, seemingly unaware that her casual comments now held the full attention of her three dinner companions.

"So come on then, out with it Monique, where did Chretien make off to with the gold. Just where would you have carted a ton of treasure off to?"

The French woman regarded Martin silently over the top of the glass she had raised to her lips, took a slow sip, and replaced the glass on the table before answering.

"Nowhere Marti, it would have been too risky. So I would not have moved it more than a few metres. I would have dropped it down the well that you mentioned."

Martin and Anna regarded her in stunned silence, then each other as the impact of Monique's casual observation registered. It was Martin who reacted first by smacking the edge of the table with the flat of his hand.

"Unbelievable."

Monique looked puzzled. "I have said something stupid?"

Anna looked across at her and said "That would make complete sense Monique. Our friend Chretien worked the whole thing out from the moment he realised that the Argenta Treasury had fallen into his lap."

"Really, you think I am right Cherie? Marti, what have you got to say?"

"Quite honestly I'm astounded Monique. All of the conclusions we told you about earlier are based on very few facts and a lot of guesswork. I don't see that the idea of the well is out of step with the rest of our theory. I can imagine that dumping the gold then dropping the dead bodies on top followed by some rubble from the walls when they slighted the fortress seemed like a perfect solution to where to hide the loot. I'll also be willing to bet that he didn't 'fill' the well with rubble either, my money will be on just a top few feet of rubble and earth beneath that. So yes Monique, I think that your idea about the well is very probably correct, and so Anna and I will return to England and talk to Grantfield University about where we can now go with this."

Although he would not have passed a breathalyser test Martin drove them back to the chateau at a sedate pace without sighting any other traffic. Once indoors they gravitated to the library and over glasses of cognac prowled again through the material that constituted their hunt for the Sarony treasure. It was Anna who voiced the feeling that appeared to have enveloped them both.

"It suddenly feels as if we have come to an end, and I'm frightened that all of this will somehow fall apart without the Sarony Treasure to hold on to."

"All of this?"

"Yes, I can't tell you my how my whole existence has changed during these past weeks, and now I'm mortally afraid that it is all dependent on some obscure balance of circumstances that will bring everything to ruins if changed."

He put both arms around the tall blond figure and crushed her so tightly against him that she could barely draw breath.

"But here in the real world Anna Freemont we may be at the end of the Sarony Treasure hunt, but the changes to your life aren't going away. We will go to Grantfield in the X3, give Smiffy our report, and you can make a decision on your career. We can commute fairly easily between Sarony and Grantfield if you decide to stay with Smiffy. If not then why not take a chance and come in with me as a freelance archaeologist? We can form our own company and work for ourselves based in Sarony. There's bags of room here at the chateau so we won't have to worry about renting offices or anything of the sort. There's an entire wing just asking to be used if necessary. If you still want to live here with me then just tell your parents and friends that you are going to get married in France and invite them to the party."

"You are absolutely certain you want to get married Martin?"

"I don't have much choice now that we have told Monique and JP. Monique will skin me alive if I try to back out. Besides which, I proposed and you said yes, and quite a few other things once we were upstairs if I recall correctly."

"You have the ability to bring out my naughty side Mr Price" she laughed.

The mood of apprehension disappeared as quickly as it had swept in and she went to the library window and looked out into the dark, remembering those evenings when she was alone and fearing the worst. She saw his image reflected in the window as he stood behind her in the room regarding her silently and she knew that she would never have to be alone again.

"It's dreadfully late," she said. "Would you like to continue this conversation upstairs?"

Chapter 28 - Smiffy

They drove onto the Grantfield campus just over a week later and Martin halted the car in one of the reserved spaces. As usual, one or two heads turned in Anna's direction when they passed through the doors into the atrium, but unusually those observers saw that the tall blonde intimidating figure of recent memory was now tightly holding the arm of a not particularly eye catching man. The large imposing indoor space was busy, but a deputation of sixth form scholars and their guide moved away from the reception desk giving Nikki-with-two-kays a clear view of the couple heading towards her. She looked down at her laptop, paused, then looked up and, without a thought for her surroundings, called out as they approached,

"I told you didn't I, bloody fantastic."

Heads turned in the direction of the commotion and observers noted that the pretty receptionist who normally greeted visitors in a quiet and friendly manner was now standing up waving her clenched fists in the air above her head.

As they reached her she added in her normal tones,

"I'll just let the Professor's secretary know you've arrived, ooh its so exciting, you two together. The ice maiden has thawed out at last, I said you should......oh!"

She sat down abruptly and the well intentioned stream of babble tailed off as Anna repeated "Ice maiden? Is that what they called me?"

Such was it's intensity, that the silence which had suddenly enveloped the immediate area of the reception desk appeared in danger of spreading throughout the entire atrium, until Martin grinned and answered Anna in clear tones that could be heard at quite some distance,

"I believe so my love. It seems that you gave off a rather cool aura, not to me of course, I've loved you from the moment you told me to fuck off."

The ludicrous comment achieved its objective and Anna's ruffled feelings evaporated as she smiled at Nikki saying,

"As you can see, Martin took your advice very much to heart, and if you would like to come to a party we are going to give in France down near Dijon, we will both be delighted to see you Nikki."

"That was very nice of you," said Martin as they made their way to the lift. "It will mean a lot to her that the invite came from you. She's good news, always treats everyone the same and she doesn't understand why you academic lot aren't more friendly. Being invited by her heroine to a posh do in France will make her ridiculously happy."

"Heroine? Come off it Martin, don't exaggerate."

"It's true. I told you. She thinks you are wonderful. Now let's see what Smiffy's got to say, he's had a couple of days to digest our report, that's assuming he managed to open the email of course."

The Professor had been equal to the task. He confirmed that he had already contacted Pavia University to ask whether it would accept the loan of a team of two from Grantfield. The remit would be very specific and only be concerned with the exploration of the Frosinone stronghold site.

"What happens if we actually turn up the treasure?" Asked Anna.

"Ah, now in that case it will be reported as a Grantfield University funded project on behalf of Pavia University. A sign of the close educational ties being fostered by myself and Dottore Francesco Borini, based on a friendship that extends back to our days as undergraduates."

He chuckled as he stretched his legs out and leaned back in his chair.

"Will we be accorded any credit as part of this academic master stroke?" Persisted Anna.

"Now that's the beauty of having good friends in high places," responded the Professor. "The two of you will have a television programme made about your hunt for and (hopefully) successful discovery of the Argenta Treasury, a joint production venture by the Italian RAI History channel and our own Channel Four. As you can see, everybody wins. Now tell me. Am I, or am I not, a genius?"

"That is the best news possible" enthused Anna "I thought we would lose out all round because of the treasure being Italian in origin and never having left Italy."

"And what about you Martin, you've not had much to say for yourself, are you satisfied with this?"

"It's a good deal Smiffy, and I am convinced that we will find the treasure, but I'm not too sure where this leaves Anna. For my own part I think the TV exposure will give me exactly what I was hoping for when I first talked it through with you, but what will her position be so far as your department is concerned?"

The Professor turned to Anna and said "The best I can do is to offer you the number two role."

"With Rod McEwan as department head?

"I'm afraid so, poor Carter won't be returning and the Welsh project will occupy a large proportion of our time and budget for the foreseeable future. In British archaeological terms it is of far greater significance than the Sarony Treasure, which has no cultural connection with this country at all."

Anna nodded and after glancing briefly at Martin replied "I understand Professor, but I will not be taking up this appointment. I will let you have my resignation as soon as we have completed the work at Frosinone. There is no way I can work in a department headed by Rod McEwan. I had feared as much, but Martin and I have come up with the idea of forming our own company to carry out archaeological research and excavation on behalf of institutions like universities. We should have a recognised pedigree in the Sarony project and, thanks to Martin's financial position, we won't need to ask for any finance. The institutions will be able to work within their set budgets because we will agree a fee in advance that will only be payable on completion of the project."

"So a flat fee for the job so to speak," mused the Professor.

"Exactly so, no open ended commitment that sucks more and more money into a project just for vanity, and the Sarony assignment is a good example of how it could work in an advantageous way on some of the more speculative projects. Grantfield is going to get a hell of a lot of publicity at virtually no cost, and all alongside its involvement in the Welsh dig."

The professor stood up, "And what do you intend to call your company?"

This time it was Martin who spoke "We thought 'Timewarp' would be appropriate, maybe a little twee but hopefully we can gain it some credibility."

"Are you sure this is the right course of action? Both of you, but you especially Anna, will be taking an enormous chance. As an elderly academic I feel qualified to point out that the field of archaeology is very competitive, at least for the big prestigious projects. You could end up high and dry and having to scuttle round doing basic site work well beneath your true abilities."

"Thanks for the advice Smiffy. I know it's well intended but Anna and I also have plans of a more personal nature that will make the chance we are taking a lot less of a gamble."

Smithson-Hunt looked from one to the other and raised an eyebrow before answering. "Well I will wish you good luck and if the opportunity arises I will offer whatever support I can."

As they re-entered the reception area a frantically waving hand caused them to veer back to the reception desk.

"Did you mean it, about coming to your party in France?" asked Nikki.

"At the risk of Anna suspecting me of trying to two-time her, if you give me your mobile number I will tell you as soon as we set a date, and book you into good accommodation" laughed Martin.

"Brilliant, oh Mr McEwan's waiting in the car park to see who has taken his parking space."

They saw him just as he saw them and Anna feared the worst as Martin said "Just go straight to the car, get in, and drive to the exit. I'll meet you there." She did as he said and saw the redhead hesitate, then turn and walk back to where his own car was waiting. With a sigh of relief she eased the X3 around to the exit and stopped to allow a grinning Martin to board. In the rear view mirror she watched Rod McEwan's car pull into her old parking space.

"So how did you know he wouldn't make a scene?"

"It's all about image with him and he's got what he wanted. It's like the Royal Standard to him. It tells the world that he's in residence and that he's not just a nobody"

"Oh, very deep, Mr Price. Did they throw in a psychology course when you were in the army?"

"They did as a matter of fact, but it's got nothing to do with psychology."

She changed gear and expertly steered the big vehicle out onto the main road leading into town before asking "What's it to do with then?"

"Just recognising a prat when you see one, and treating him accordingly, hey watch it." He added the last comment as Anna burst out laughing and almost mounted the pavement as she punched him in the shoulder.

Chapter 29 - Vera

The party finally took place at the beginning of September when the weather retained a comfortable warmth and the leaves still held fast to their precarious high level anchorages. The fir trees provided their usual year round green screen separating the estate from the world at large, and Martin had let it be known that all local residents were welcome. Having read that in past years it had been traditional for the Sarony family to host an annual fair for the village he decided to reinstate the event, and so when the UK guests arrived they found a Summer Fair laid on as part of the entertainment.

All visitors were allowed access to the family vault, and a continual trickle found their way down the now uncovered steps through the newly installed oak door and into the cool, dimly lit interior. Although trouble was not expected there were a number of off-duty police operating as a general security measure under the watchful eye of Jean-Paul who was, in any event, a named guest for the family dinner arranged for the evening. Martin kept his promise to Nikki Prendergast who, like Anna's parents, had mystifyingly been ordered to arrive a few days earlier. To her delight Nikki found herself ensconced in one of the chateau's guest bedrooms with Anna's parents in another, and Professor Smithson-Hunt and his wife in yet another. Bertrand and Emilia completed the chateau guest list. Marcel and 'Etta had to be almost forcibly restrained from working, with Martin insisting that they were guests and that a dim view would be taken if they were spotted wandering around armed with trays of drinks.

The select group invited to attend 48 hours in advance of the party date found themselves present at a unique event the day after their arrival. Together with Monique, Jean-Paul, two large friends of Martin's, and the Moranes they made up the congregation attending the wedding of Martin and Anna. The ceremony was conducted in the open air on the site of the old chapel. This, as the happy couple explained, was a small gesture to acknowledge the major part played by Chretien de Sarony and his tragic family in bringing them together.

For Martin there was the nerve wracking experience of a first meeting with Anna's parents and, despite an excellent wedding supper at Auberge Fleurie, he still felt unusually awkward by the time of the fair the following day. Her mother was what is generally known as 'not an easy woman' and was not at all happy at having the news of her only child's wedding sprung upon her once she was stranded in France. She had only agreed to attend the party in order to satisfy her curiosity regarding Anna's boyfriend, and how it was that he appeared to own a French chateau. Having to explain to her friends back home that she knew nothing of her daughter's wedding plans was as bad at having to pretend that she had known all along but hadn't told them. She hadn't yet decided which course of action was the more socially acceptable. Then there was Anna's husband Martin who, although ticking the boxes marking him as well brought up, comfortably off, and apparently a mentally stable white

Anglo-Saxon, nonetheless had an air about him that made her feel vaguely uncomfortable.

His two friends from home were both disconcertingly of a similar ilk. They were both nice enough fellows, affable well mannered and solidly built, but again with a certain something that made her feel a little on edge whenever she spoke to them.

Anna's father was less tightly buttoned than his wife. He was an old fashioned academic style of headmaster and hit it off immediately with Martin's friend 'Smiffy' who, to his surprise, turned out to be Professor Smithson-Hunt and Anna's boss at the university. He had adored his daughter from the moment she was born and could see from the way in which his new son-in-law looked at her that he could now hand this baton safely to a new admirer.

Despite his quiet and cultivated demeanour, Gordon Freemont still had an eye for a good looking woman. He was happy to stroll amongst the visitors at the fair, admiring the many stylish French girls on display in their summer clothes, and revisiting happy memories of his youth. It was with some surprise even so, that he found himself accosted by the particularly attractive young woman named Monique, whom he had been briefly introduced to before the wedding and apparently was partner with Martin in the village auberge. To his delight she linked arms with him and insisted that he accompanied her on the lengthy walk through the grounds to the family vault and back. By the time he rejoined his wife, and Monique had disappeared on some mission to do with the afternoon's festivities, he was feeling at least ten years younger than when he had got out of bed that morning.

Smithson-Hunt and his wife had spent most of the afternoon at the family vault partly out of natural and professional curiosity, and also as a means of keeping Vera Freemont at a safe distance. This was mainly due to her persistent attempts to investigate Martin's social background, and also to her relentless interrogation regarding their own social circle.

At four o'clock in the afternoon an announcement was made, via the sound system rigged up on the front lawn, asking for all present to kindly spare a moment and gather for an important announcement. A crowd duly assembled, and a team of waiters and waitresses bearing glasses of champagne hurried amongst the throng while Monique caught many a male eye – but made a point of smiling at Gordon Freemont- as she stepped forward onto the temporary stage. She made a short speech in French and then English stating that she was happy to announce that following a ceremony two days earlier Chateau Sarony now had both a master and mistress whose intention it was to make the chateau their permanent home. Martin and Anna then stepped forward and raised their glasses to the crowd and several gallons of champagne quickly met it's pre-ordained fate to the strains of the La Marseillaise

Dinner that evening was a resounding success with the mixture of nationalities getting along surprisingly well. Monique became the life and soul of the party, much to the delight of Rob Montague and Ian Donaldson, Martin's friends from his army days. They reminded Anna very much of her new husband with their quiet yet obviously strong characters and high intelligence. She also noticed that any questions relating to their service lives were either answered in a bland manner or skilfully deflected so that no great detail was revealed.

Intriguingly she noted that they appeared to be on familiar terms with Jean-Paul and, like Martin, could speak French fluently. The nearest she came to finding out anything of interest occurred at a point when there was an unexpected lull in the hilarity Monique was causing in conjunction with Nikki. She suddenly tuned in to hear Ian say to Martin,

"No more problems with those biker characters I take it?"

"No, they won't be back, but your offer to come over was much appreciated."

"Any time skipper, you know that. But I guess with JP here as well it was always under control."

At that moment a great shout of laughter erupted from the other end of the table, and that was the last Anna heard pass between them in reference to Martin's past.

The evening moved on, the wine flowed and then suddenly people began to say goodnight. Thierry collected Monique and the two old army friends who were staying at the auberge. It had been a tremendous day and the last thing Anna said as she crawled zombie-like into bed was "I've never felt so tired, no hanky panky for us." An answering snore confirmed the unanimity of the decision.

The following morning started late and for Anna in a particularly baffling fashion. No sooner had she shakily poured herself a coffee than her mother sidled up to her and hissed conspiratorially, "Anna darling, your father had the most extraordinary conversation with one of Martin's friends last night."

Still not entirely one with the world at large Anna unthinkingly mumbled "That's nice Mummy" as she refilled her coffee cup. This was completely the wrong answer and Vera Freemont swiftly went onto the offensive.

"No Anna, it's not nice, not nice at all. Apparently Martin got annoyed with some French lads recently, and not only hung them upside down from a bridge but painted their..um, well painted their private parts red."

"Yes Mummy I know."

"You know? Don't you mind?"

"Provided he doesn't do the same to me no, not really."

Mrs Freemont was appalled "Don't be disgusting darling, and that's not all."

"Oh God."

"The English girl whose got the room next to ours."

"Nikki with...... er Prendergast."

"Yes dear, well from some of the sounds I heard before I went to sleep last night, and again this morning, I can tell you she didn't spend the night alone"

"No Mummy, she spent it with JP."

"That French policeman? But he must be twenty years older than her."

"Well, if I'd met JP when I went away for a weekend with friends, I wouldn't have said no!"

There was a long and strained silence as Mrs Freemont stared at her daughter before saying "You've changed Anna."

"I am sure I have Mummy, but that is because having met Martin I know that if Nikki is having similar feelings about JP, then she's welcome to keep him locked in that bedroom for the rest of the week."

At this moment Anna's father entered the kitchen and Anna, who had endured her mother's prattling thanks only to the fortifying qualities of the coffee bean, took the opportunity to draw him into the conversation.

"Hello Daddy, did you sleep well?"

"Like a log dear. Very interesting man your husband, I mean for an archaeologist, that is. Well what I mean is, one of those, um, rather muscular friends of his was telling me they spent some time in the army with him, not sure doing what exactly. Had a bit more to drink than usual last night." This admission earned him a very hard stare from his wife, but he affected not to notice and continued, "Yes, apparently there is a particular technique to use when being attacked with a knife and Martin was rather an expert it seems. Obviously it was all er practice, but even so....."

Anna was aware of her mother's obvious disapproval and couldn't resist saying "Yes Daddy, but having broken the attacker's arm, it's a good idea to knee him in the face as hard as possible so that he doesn't do it again."

She had the satisfaction of hearing her mother say "Oh my God" just as a roar of laughter announced Martin's entry to the kitchen with Nikki Prendergast firmly clutched in his grasp. "Well you tell JP that you are our honoured guest, and if he wants to lure you away to his place over at Duclos he has to ask my permission. You can't trust these French coppers young Nikki, oh you know that already of course. 'morning all, sleep well did you? Where's the coffee? Don't know what Smiffy's going to say. Hello my love, young Nikki here is just going to take JP up some coffee, he's exhausted apparently. Can't think why, can you Nik?"

A giggling and still slightly dishevelled Nikki busied herself with the coffee as Anna grabbed Martin's shirt front and laughingly pulled him against her.

"Now that you've put Nikki down why don't you tell us what you are talking about Martin. I think your new 'in-laws' are wondering what sort of people I've got involved with."

Martin confiscated the coffee Nikki had just poured for JP and turned to face Anna's parents.

"You met Smiffy - Anna's prof - and his wife of course"

"Oh, Professor Smithson-Hunt" replied Vera Freemont."

"That's the chap, well first of all he sees me kidnap Anna into a life of lust and debauchery, and now his favourite receptionist from the University has decided to run riot with the French gendarmerie. Excuse me one moment." He turned and addressed Nikki who was heading out of the kitchen with a replacement cup of coffee. "Tell JP I need a word after you've had your evil way with him Nik."

"I already have and it wasn't evil" giggled Nikki and winked at an aghast Mrs Freemont as she exited with the coffee.

Turning back to a dumbstruck Vera Freemont he careered on "So you see, my old mate Smiffy is bound to hold me responsible for the, well, the um…" His stream of good humoured banter hit the buffers as he realised for the first time that Anna's mother was operating on a less earthy wavelength. Hastily Martin put his arm around Anna's shoulders and said "Don't worry you two, Lady Anna here is in safe hands, and Nikki is nobody's fool. JP is going to find his off-duty life a little more lively than he's grown used to since, er …… since he joined the constabulary."

He detached himself from Anna and taking her mother by the arm said "Now Vera, let me take you for a personal tour of the gardens, and tell you how I came to fall for your beautiful daughter. Have you ever heard of Armand Furneaux, the famous archaeologist?"

A bemused Vera Freemont allowed herself to be gently steered out of the kitchen and onto the rear terrace as Anna smiled apologetically at her father.

"Let's rustle up some breakfast Daddy, and I'll tell you how I've ended up this happy."

END

Proof

Made in the USA
Charleston, SC
05 June 2016